PENGUIN BOOKS

MORE RUMOR!

Hal Morgan was born in 1954 and graduated from Hampshire College. He is the author of *Symbols of America*, and co-author of *Amazing 3-D* and *Prairie Fires and Paper Moons: The American Photographic Postcard, 1900–1920*. Kerry Tucker was born in Connecticut in 1955, raised in Youngstown, Ohio, and educated at Chatham College in Pittsburgh and Northeastern University School of Law. She is the author of two other books, *Greetings from New York: A Visit to Manhattan in Postcards* and *Greetings from Los Angeles: A Visit to the City of Angels in Postcards*. Morgan and Tucker have previously collaborated on *Rumor!* and *The Shower Songbook*.

MORE RUMOR!

Hal Morgan and
Kerry Tucker

A Steam Press Book

PENGUIN BOOKS

PENGUIN BOOKS

Viking Penguin Inc., 40 West 23rd Street,
New York, New York 10010, U.S.A.
Penguin Books Ltd, Harmondsworth,
Middlesex, England
Penguin Books Australia Ltd, Ringwood,
Victoria, Australia
Penguin Books Canada Limited, 2801 John Street,
Markham, Ontario, Canada L3R 1B4
Penguin Books (N.Z.) Ltd, 182–190 Wairau Road,
Auckland 10, New Zealand

First published in Penguin Books 1987
Published simultaneously in Canada

Copyright © Steam Press, 1987
All rights reserved

Printed in the United States of America by
Offset Paperback Inc., Dallas, Pennsylvania

MORE
RUMOR!

INTRODUCTION

WHY IS IT that rumors thrive best in the dark? Since the publication of our first book about rumors (*Rumor!*) in 1984 we've been asked to participate in countless radio call-in sessions—at all times of the day and night. But at night, and especially during the earliest morning hours, callers feel free to bare their most private thoughts to strangers. "My sister-in-law says that Ida Lupino was totally bald. Is this true?" "My father was in the navy, and he says that the military created a time warp in Philadelphia during World War II. What do you know about that?"

It's humbling to be expected to know the answers to absolutely everything. And since we of course don't know all the answers, we've been forced many times to respond to callers with, "We don't know, but we'll find out." This book is the result of all that finding out.

Generous readers of *Rumor!* have swamped our mailbox with questions about new rumors, variations on old ones, and speculation about the origins of the most elusive ones. When Michael Jackson had his brush with flames in 1984 during the filming of the notorious Pepsi commercial, readers and radio callers were quick to tell us about the toll-free number (1-800-MICHAEL, according to most reports) that we could call in order to console him. Not surprisingly, the number didn't work. The same commercial fueled yet another widespread and untrue story—that the child breakdancer who performed in the commercial had died of a broken neck.

The rumors that we've been alerted to and explore in *More Rumor!* fall more or less into the traditional categories. "Conspiracy" rumors are all around us: many radio callers have told us that NASA has proved the existence of a lost day mentioned in the Bible, but has conspired with the government to keep the revelation from the public. Other readers have told us of the untrue rumor that the FCC plans to ban religious broadcasting.

The category of "shocking celebrity stories" is a bottomless well of scandal and peculiarity: rumor has it (incorrectly) that Clint Eastwood is Stan Laurel's son and that George Reeves, TV's Superman, fell to his death while attempting to fly. (He did not.)

We continue to hear shocking stories about products, too. When a novel product becomes successful, rumormongers tend to devise stories that point out the product's tragic flaw. The implication is that nothing can be *that* good. Examples include the untrue rumors that a butane lighter in a welder's pocket was hit by a spark and exploded with the force of three sticks of dynamite, that Jockey shorts make men sterile, and that a woman used super-bonding glue to attach her husband's penis to his leg.

In *Rumor!* we discussed the prediction that Elvis Presley would return from the dead in 1985. As far as we know, he didn't. But that genre of rumors—the "resurrection" rumor—continues to flourish, along with its companion genre—that certain celebrities never really died at all, but went into hiding in remote places. Mass denial of tragic events is certainly understandable. What isn't understandable are the unlikely locations where rumormongers place the not-dead celebrities: Marilyn Monroe is rumored to be waiting on tables in Alaska, and a disfigured Glenn Miller is rumored to be hiding in France.

"Something for nothing" stories are favorites among students of rumor—perhaps because they are so childlike in tone. In addition to the rumors involving seeing-eye dogs for gum-wrapper chains and Ford cars for pennies that we discussed in *Rumor!*, we've come across a grisly story of the same genre: that you can sell your body *in advance* to Harvard Medical School for $500. These stories seem to satisfy something like a primeval urge to make a silk purse from a sow's ear. People who tell us these stories always tell them with the same wistful expressions on their faces, even when they admit that they know the stories aren't true.

Rumors concerning satanism continue to enthrall the gullible and the fearful. After several years of combating the untrue rumor that their 134-year-old moon-and-stars trademark was a sign of devil worship, Procter & Gamble decided to remove the mark from its products in 1985. Despite the company's patient, expensive truth-telling campaign, the rumor had refused to die.

Spreaders of Satan-related rumors have recently targeted rock groups, including the groups AC/DC and Kiss. And according to one recent and truly bizarre rumor, the theme song from the television show "Mr. Ed," when played backward, reveals a satanic message. Although most of these rumors can be shrugged off as simply silly, "devil-worship" rumors of the kind that dogged Procter & Gamble are a twentieth-century incarnation of the witch-hunt made even more frightening because rumors can spread so quickly through mass-communications systems.

Other rumors defeat any attempt at classification. We call these "amazing-story" rumors. These are outlandish yarns, related with enough detail to lend them a tone of authenticity, that appear to be told simply to get a gasp of disbelief, or disgust, or delight from the listener. They include the rumors that sewers across the country flood during commercial breaks in the Super Bowl, that an excess of "blackout" babies were born just nine months after the New York City blackout, and that a draftee was rejected by the army because he had an obscenity tattooed on his saluting finger. These rumors are told simply for entertainment's sake. Like most rumors, they are all but impossible to trace, having been relayed by a best friend's cousin, who heard it from his dentist. Such stories often pick up new characters, ironies, and subplots in the retelling.

Where do rumors come from? Why do people tell them? Even though constant entertainment is available to most people at the flick of a radio or television switch, and even though newspapers and magazines teem with genuine dramas, most people simply cannot resist the urge to tell a good story that *isn't* in the news. These stories put people on the inside—they make us feel special and in the know. What's more, rumors reveal aspects of our culture that we tend not to dwell on: at their worst they reflect our most peculiar paranoias and our darkest desires; at their most inventive they reflect our silliest fantasies and our love of the absurd.

★ ★ Seeds found in ancient Egyptian tombs sprouted when planted by archaeologists and grew into long-extinct varieties of wheat. (1890s)

Not true, although a heated scientific discussion about the possibility of growing "mummy wheat" raged during the late nineteenth century. Many reputable scientists and nurserymen grew seeds that they believed came directly from containers found in ancient tombs, but most of their successes were later found to be the result of mix-ups with modern seeds.

In 1894, at the height of the dispute, an English gardener grew a crop of healthy oats from seeds found in a mummy case given to the Duke of Sutherland by the khedive of Egypt (the Turkish governor of the country). An expert at the Royal Botanic Garden, however, examined some of the seeds and found them to be no more than two years old. A closer check of the mummy case turned up some gaps in the joints, and then it was discovered that the khedive had stored the case in his stables along with oats for his horses. For good measure, the royal botanist pointed out that oats had not even been grown in Egypt at the time of the mummy's burial.

Many other gardeners were confused by a variety of wheat widely grown in Egypt and called "mummy wheat" because it resembled plants depicted in tomb paintings. Tourists who brought mummy-wheat seeds back from Egypt often thought they were planting ancient grain, when in fact the seeds were quite fresh.

Though scientists have yet to find an authentic specimen of live mummy wheat from an ancient tomb, they have discovered some amazingly durable seeds from other sources. Certain legumes have grown after more than 150 years of storage in museum collections, and a water lily, *Nelumbium speciosum*, sprouted after 250 years. A Japanese botanist found some viable lotus seeds buried in peat in a dry lake bed in Manchuria. Germination tests yielded plants from almost all the seeds, and carbon 14 dating put the seeds' age at between eight hundred and twelve hundred years.

★ ★ Well-preserved specimens of the long-extinct wooly mammoth have been found frozen in Siberia. Scientists plan to clone a live animal from the frozen cells. (1980)

True. A Russian gold prospector discovered an amazingly well-preserved baby mammoth in 1977; it was embedded in permafrost in a remote mountainous region of northeastern Siberia. Just seven months old when it died, the little mammoth had lain frozen underground for forty thousand years. Scientists carefully removed the body from the frozen ground and shipped it to the Zoological Institute in Leningrad for further study. It was the first intact mammoth discovered since

14

1839 and the first to be examined using modern scientific techniques. Another nearly intact mammoth had been found in 1900, but, by the time it had been excavated and brought to Leningrad (then St. Petersburg) for study, it had begun to decompose. When Czar Nicholas II and the czarina came to see it in the steam-heated zoological museum, its "repulsive ammoniacal stench" drove them quickly to the other end of the building.

The 1977 specimen had never been thawed, and therefore it remained in much better condition than any previous find. Both Russian and American scientists studied samples from various parts of the mammoth's body, hoping to find active proteins within the cells. Allan C. Wilson, an evolutionary biochemist at the University of California at Berkeley, was one of the first Americans to look at the mammoth tissue. He found no active proteins but was able to glean some valuable information about the animal's evolutionary history.

The Russian scientists were more ambitious. In 1980, Vladimir Chernigovsky of the Soviet Academy of Sciences announced that efforts were under way to make a culture of living mammoth cells. If successful, "the final stage of the experiment—creation of a living specimen of the prehistoric northern elephant—would be completely feasible." Initial efforts to find living cells had been disappointing, admitted other scientists working on the project, but, if a culture could be made, a cell nucleus could then be inserted into a fertilized elephant egg and implanted in the

the womb of a female elephant. According to the plan, the elephant would then give birth to a baby wooly mammoth eighteen to twenty months later. To date, all efforts to find live genetic material in the mammoth's cells have been unsuccessful.

In addition to encouraging hopes for the revival of a species, the discovery of the frozen mammoth has also given rise to fears of ancient disease. When the body was first shipped to Leningrad, it had to be accompanied by a veterinary certificate stating that it was not a danger to the public health. And tissue samples coming to the United States for study have had to be kept in sterile isolation because of official fears that they might contain bacteria too powerful for modern antibiotics to combat. Those fears have proved unfounded, as no disease-causing bacteria has been found in any of the mammoth tissue.

★ ★ In the nineteenth century, a shortage of raw materials led a New England paper manufacturer to experiment with fiber from Egyptian mummies. He imported several shiploads of mummies and made a few successful batches of paper from the linen wrappings. But he soon discovered an unforeseen hazard. Several of his workers, charged with stripping the wrappings from the corpses, died of an ancient form of cholera, reactivated after thousands of years by moisture on the workers' hands. (1940s)

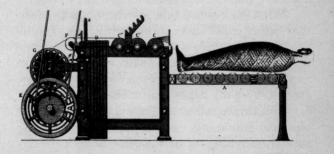

Unconfirmed. This story has long been a popular one in the paper and printing business, and in the last few years it has been given far wider play in magazine articles about the growing scarcity of mummies. The ancient bodies are now of great interest to scientists studying diet, disease, and health trends through history, and the old tale of the mummy paper is sometimes called on to dramatize appeals to save the mummies for scientific research. Aidan Cockburn, for instance, in the introduction to his book *Mummies, Disease and Ancient Cultures* (1980) states

17

that thousands of mummies were used in Canada in the nineteenth century for the manufacture of paper. Reviews of Cockburn's book picked up on the story as a lively tidbit, and other scientists have since relied on it as fact. We have found the story repeated in such diverse publications as *Omni* (February 1986), *Scientific American* (November 1981), and the *Boston Globe Magazine* (June 1, 1986). Unfortunately, there is no reliable evidence that any paper manufacturer really used mummy wrappings as a source of fiber, and the story has all the earmarks of a spicy rumor.

What makes the tale interesting is the fact that paper mills in the nineteenth century did use huge quantities of cloth rags in the manufacture of paper. Until the 1870s, when practical methods of making paper from wood were discovered, almost all paper was made from recycled rags. And since collecting the rags was both troublesome and costly, mill operators were constantly searching for new sources of fiber.

The story of the mummy paper can probably be traced to Dard Hunter's book *Papermaking: The History and Technique of an Ancient Craft*, first published in 1943. Hunter's book has been widely read through the years as an authoritative history of papermaking, and one of its most intriguing passages follows the heading "Stanwood and His Mummy Paper." Hunter explains that I. Augustus Stanwood may have been one of the first American manufacturers to make paper from wood, in 1863 at his Maine paper mill. Hunter goes on to say that Stanwood may also have made paper from mummies:

The information here set down regarding the mummy paper was given to me by Stanwood's son, Daniel, a retired professor of international law, living in Massachusetts. During the Civil War, according to Professor Stanwood, his father was pressed for raw material to keep the Maine mill in operation and he had to use his ingenuity to overcome the difficulty. This he did by importing mummies from Egypt for the sole purpose of stripping the dried bodies of their cloth wrappings and using the material for making paper. Professor Stanwood informed me that his father brought several shiploads of mummies to his mill in Gardiner, Maine, and threw the woven wrappings as well as the papyrus filling into beaters and manufactured a coarse brown wrapping paper, which eventually found its way into the shops of grocers, butchers, and other merchants who used paper of this kind. It was further stated that the rags stripped from the long-dead Egyptians caused an epidemic of cholera among the rag-pickers and cutters in the Maine mill, for at that period there was no regulation regarding the disinfection of rags. Professor Stanwood also related that the only competition his father encountered in purchasing the mummies was the Egyptian railroad, for during a ten-year period the locomotives of Egypt made use of no other fuel than that furnished by the well-wrapped, compact mummies, the supply of which was thought at the time to be almost unlimited.

Hunter was clearly intrigued by the tale, and he used it effectively to liven up his history, but he treated it with the arm's-length respect due a family tale recounted some eighty years after the fact. Professor Stanwood's account may indeed be true, but he casts serious doubt on it with the flourish about the Egyptian railroad's use of mummies as fuel, a tale that is almost certainly legend. Mark Twain told the same story in his satirical travelogue, *Innocents Abroad*, published in 1875. Twain's book is full of absurd exaggerations and untruths, delivered in his typical straight-faced style, and among them he includes the story of the mummies burned on the Egyptian railroad:

> I shall only say that the fuel they use for the locomotive is composed of mummies three thousand years old, purchased by the ton or by the graveyard for the purpose, and that sometimes one hears the profane engineer call out pettishly, "D—n these plebeians, they don't burn worth a cent—pass out a King." (Stated to me for a fact. I only tell it as I got it. I am willing to believe it. I can believe anything.)

Though Twain was obviously writing farce rather than fact, even today his passage is cited as evidence of the wanton abuse of mummies.

Dard Hunter did do some further investigation into the possibility that mummy wrappings were used to make paper, and he uncovered a couple of other tantalizing leads. In 1855 a New York scientist, Isaiah Deck, wrote a paper suggesting that mummy wrappings might be a profitable source of fiber for American papermakers. Deck pointed out that paper mills consumed over two hundred thousand tons of rags each year, and that the demand for paper was outgrowing the supply of rags. According to Deck, a huge supply of mummies lay buried in the sands of Egypt, wrapped in valuable quantities of linen. In addition to the linen on the human corpses, he pointed to the cloth on the mummies of "the sacred bulls, crocodiles, ibises, and cats," estimating that up to thirty pounds of fabric could be pulled from each specimen. As to the economics of mummy paper, Deck estimated that mummy wrappings would cost under three cents a pound, compared to five cents for ordinary rags.

In the August 19, 1856, edition of the Syracuse, New York, *Daily Standard* Hunter found an editorial chastising a papermaker from Onondaga County for selling "paper made from the wrappings of mummies." The writer was outraged by the manufacturer's lack of respect for the dead, charging that "he would pass the cerements of Cleopatra through a paper mill as quick as he would the shirt of Winnebago." The essay is intriguing, but no further evidence of the mummy paper has been found. The writer may well have been reacting to a rumor. When the Syracuse *Post-Standard* reprinted the editorial in 1940, in response to renewed curiosity about mummy paper, one woman wrote the paper with a recollection of another version of the tale. She had been told the story about forty years earlier by a friend of her father, Dr. Myron K. Waite:

> Dr. Waite said that when he was a young man (about 1855–1860) he worked in a paper mill in Broadalbin where they received great bundles of old linen wrappings from Egyptian mummies, which they made into paper. He said that the rolled-up vestments retained the shape of the mummy, so that when the workmen tried to straighten or unroll the "cocoon," as it might be called, it sprang back at once into the shape of the mummy it had encased so long.

While Dr. Waite may have worked with mummy

wrappings at a paper mill, the embellishments on the story almost certainly place it in the realm of rumor and legend.

At a distance of more than a hundred years, it is difficult to find anything conclusive about paper made from mummy wrappings. It is possible that small quantities of paper were made from the wrappings on an experimental basis. But Egyptologists we spoke with at Boston's Museum of Fine Arts and the University of Pennsylvania's University Museum of Archaeology/Anthropology doubt that shiploads of mummies could ever have been imported to make commercial quantities of paper.

We can discount the legend of the ancient strain of cholera reactivated by the moisture from workers' hands. Bacteria could not survive a year in the arid conditions of an Egyptian tomb, much less the centuries suggested by the legend. When scientists recently discovered that the mummy of Ramses V is covered with small blisters characteristic of smallpox, some worried that those handling ancient corpses should be vaccinated against the disease. In a letter to the *Journal of the American Medical Association* (June 7, 1985), Dr. Peter Lewin dismisses the concern, stating that there is absolutely no danger of catching smallpox from dried mummies.

★ ★ If you ever run short of cash, you can sell your body to the Harvard Medical School for $500. They will tattoo the bottom of your foot "Property of Harvard Medical School," and upon your death your body will immediately be shipped to the school for dissection. (1940s)

Not true. The Harvard Medical School does not buy its bodies, and it never has, according to David Gunner, Coordinator of Anatomical Gifts at Harvard. The school relies entirely on donations from people who specify in their wills that they wish their bodies to go to the school and whose wishes are supported by surviving relatives. In spite of this policy, the school receives several calls a week from people seeking the rumored cash advance.

Gunner points out that buying bodies would be bad business, as nothing would prevent the seller from leaving the country with the money, or from dying in such a way as to make the body useless to the school—in a fire, for instance, or in a bad automobile accident. The school can only use intact corpses that can be easily transported to its facilities.

The story probably has its roots in the practices of eighteenth- and nineteenth-century anatomy schools. Before the state recognized the legitimate need of doctors to learn about the human body from the study of actual corpses, private anatomy schools often operated in a secretive manner to avoid conflict with the law. These schools could not openly arrange for the donation of bodies, so they had to rely on other means of supply. Grave robbing was not unheard of; the fear of it prompted some to bury loved ones under "robber-proof" iron grates. And it is likely that bodies were sometimes purchased from workers who had access to corpses in city morgues. Tales of this body trade may have evolved over the years into the modern medical-school legend.

The money-for-your-body story may also have sprung spontaneously from the same well of wishful thinking that has spawned other "money for nothing" stories, such as the belief that Revlon will pay for fingernail clippings (they won't; see *Rumor!*, page 46) or that the Ford Motor Company will give a free car to anyone who finds a 1943 copper penny (they won't; see *Rumor!*, page 38). Like those stories, the Harvard legend somehow lends the world an element of optimism and magic that it really doesn't have. It's comforting to believe that Harvard would pay us for our bodies if we were ever really strapped. We used to believe this ourselves, and we hate to be the ones to break the bad news. We hope our tough realism will prompt readers to make better financial back-up plans.

★ ★ If you write to the Heinz food company just before your fifty-seventh birthday, they will send you a free carton of Heinz products. (1960s)

True at one time. Until the 1950s, Heinz did send free cases of food to anyone who wrote of a coming fifty-seventh birthday. No questions were asked. But the practice has been discontinued, according to a company representative, because the number fifty-seven is not as important to Heinz now that it sells hundreds of products.

We suspect that the reason may have more to do with the cost of sending out free food, as fifty-seven still seems to be a magic number at Heinz. The company still sells Heinz 57 sauce, it prints the "57 Varieties" slogan on all its labels, its address is Post Office Box 57 in Pittsburgh, and its main telephone number ends in 5757.

Curiously, the number fifty-seven never had anything to do with the number of products made by the company. H. J. Heinz came up with the "57 Varieties" slogan in 1896 when he noticed a sign over a shoe store advertising "21 Styles." At the time his firm made more than sixty different products, but Heinz settled on fifty-seven as a catchy number, and he rushed to a print shop to order streetcar ads promoting his "57 Varieties."

H. J. Heinz's son, Henry John Heinz II, has carried on the birthday-gift program in a limited way, occasionally recognizing the fifty-seventh birthday of a friend with a case of Heinz food. The founder's grandson, Senator John Heinz (R., Pa.), does not make a practice of giving away Heinz products.

★ ★ There is a secret underground city beneath Manhattan, accessible only by special elevators that are directed by a code pressed on the elevator buttons.

Unconfirmed. We admit to a secret fondness for this rumor, though deep in our hearts we know it isn't true. But what if there really is such a city, even better than the city above ground? What if we just don't know the right people and haven't yet been admitted to the inner circle that is allowed to go there? It is a fantasy a six-year-old might have, of a secret place open only to a select few.

There are some underground shopping arcades in New York City that the average tourist might not discover on a quick visit, but none of these can really be called secret. Visitors who come by subway to the World Trade Center will find a mall of shops not visible from the street. The Citicorp building also has a shopping arcade at its base, but it would be hard to miss, as it extends up to the ground level. Less apparent are the shops and restaurants beneath Rockefeller Center, which almost do form a miniature underground city. This underground shopping center was built primarily to serve the workers in the skyscrapers of Rockefeller Center, who can go there by elevator in bad weather and never have to step outside. Rockefeller Center was also built with hidden underground loading docks, so that trucks making deliveries do not clog traffic in the area. Through an unobtrusive street-level entrance, trucks drive down a winding track to reach the loading area, some three floors beneath the bustle of the street.

Washington, D.C., also has a development with concealed underground restaurants and shops. Crystal City, between the Pentagon and National Airport, looks from the street to be a sterile collection of office towers with only a few stores. One floor down, however, is a ten-block shopping area, including a supermarket, a movie theater, several restaurants, and dozens of small stores. Here the real secrets are above ground, however. We once took the wrong elevator up and when we stepped off found ourselves surrounded by military uniforms. We were quickly shown the down button.

━━━━━━━━━━━━━━━━━━━━━━━━

★ ★ There is a secret city in Russia built to look just like an American town. The people there speak English with a perfect American accent and learn American ways in preparation for spy work in the United States. (1960s)

Unconfirmed. This is a curiously appealing story for which there is no factual evidence. We'd love to see the city if it exists and to find out just how far they go in copying our culture. Do they eat peanut butter and jelly sandwiches, Twinkies, and Moon Pies? Do they watch "The

Price Is Right" and "Dallas" on television? Are they allowed to see the *Rambo* films?

It certainly is in Russia's interest to train foreign diplomats and spies who can adapt comfortably to another nation's way of life, just as it is in the United States' interest to send diplomats abroad who can communicate well in the language of their host countries. The story of the American training city in Russia has probably grown out of personal encounters with Russians who speak fluent English with an American accent. One correspondent who first heard the story at Expo 67 in Montreal attached it to a particular Russian journalist. On his first trip out of Russia, the man "spoke English like my relatives in Buffalo," and many assumed he'd received secret training. Since the idea of learning a foreign language to perfection seems an awesome task to us, we are often surprised by the fluency of foreigners.

We suspect that there is no American city in Russia, but that there probably are intensive language-training centers there, just as there are in the United States. One of the most effective ways to learn a language well is to speak it day in and day out for a period of weeks, until the mind stops translating each word and begins to think comfortably in the second language.

★ ★ The guillotine was named for its inventor, who became one of the first to be beheaded by the machine during the French Revolution. (1800)

Not true. Joseph Ignace Guillotin, a respected physician and a member of France's National Assembly, proposed in 1789 that hanging be abolished as a form of capital punishment and that decapitation be used instead. At the time only nobles and those of high rank were given the benefit of beheading, while people of lower birth were subjected to the rope. Dr. Guillotin also suggested that future decapitations be carried out "by means of a simple mechanism." His proposal was made for humanitarian reasons; he thought beheading the fastest and least painful means of execution, and he hoped a machine would eliminate the clumsy mistakes and extended suffering that sometimes went with death by the sword.

Dr. Guillotin did not invent the machine that eventually took his name, and he did not die under its blade. Beheading devices had been in use in Europe since the fourteenth century. One was used in 1307 in Ireland, and others may have been in use even earlier in Germany, Italy, and England. A beheading machine known as "the maiden" was still widely used in Europe when Guillotin made his proposal. When the National Assembly finally voted for Dr. Guillotin's decapitation machine in 1791, the job of designing it was given to Dr. Antoine Louis, secretary of the Academy of Medicine.

Dr. Louis's first device was built by a German named Tobias Schmidt and was dubbed the "louisette" or "louison." (One legend holds that Louis XVI, who would become the machine's best-known casualty, suggested the distinctive angled blade to Dr. Louis. No evidence exists to support the story.) The first victim of the new equipment was a highwayman named Peletier, who was executed on April 22, 1792. Over the next several years, as the blade's human toll climbed higher and higher, the public began to reassociate the machine with Dr. Guillotin. Songs were written about the doctor and his speech before the National Assembly, and before long the "louisette" began to be called the "guillotine."

Dr. Louis himself fell victim to the guillotine during the Reign of Terror, and his death may be at the root of the legend of Dr. Guillotin's execution. The story may also have started when Guillotin was condemned to die for supporting enemies of Robespierre. He was only spared by a change of government that sent Robespierre instead to the guillotine.

Dr. Guillotin survived the Revolution, though he lived out his life stigmatized by his connection with the slaughtering machine. He finally died in 1814 of a carbuncle on his shoulder. Soon afterward his children petitioned the government for the right to change their last name.

★ ★ The Lamborghini automobile company was started in reaction to a personal snub by Enzo Ferrari. Industrial tycoon Ferruccio Lamborghini stopped in at the Ferrari headquarters to request a special alteration to his sports car. When the company president refused to see him, Lamborghini angrily decided to launch a competing car business. His bull trademark is a deliberate jab at Ferrari's horse emblem. (1967)

Not true. Ferruccio Lamborghini's dissatisfaction with the leading sports car models of the early 1960s did prompt him to enter the automobile market. His decision was not based on anger, however, but rather on a businessman's perception of a niche in the market waiting to be filled.

Lamborghini started his first business venture in 1946, converting surplus army vehicles into farm machines. A year later he began to dabble in automobile conversions. He took a used Fiat Topolino, added a powerful new engine with a bronze cylinder head, and turned it into a race car. For some months he kept his workers busy modifying engines for other Fiat owners. In 1948 he dropped the car work to concentrate on tractors, and over the next decade built up a sizable manufacturing business. From tractors, Lamborghini expanded into heating equipment, and, finally, in 1963, with the finances of his tractor and heating operations to back him up, he decided to make the ultimate luxury sports car. Announcing his decision, he explained, "In the past I have bought some of the most famous *gran tourismo* cars and in each of these magnificent machines I have found some faults. Too hot, or uncomfortable, or not sufficiently fast or not perfectly finished. Now I want to make a *gran tourismo* car without faults. Not a technical bomb. Very normal, very conventional, but a perfect car." He chose his birth sign, Taurus the bull, as a symbol for the new automobile.

The legend of the sports car's origin in a personal argument is actually a modern reincarnation of a story that has been around in the automobile industry for decades. James W. Packard is said to have had the same fight with the head of the Winton car company back in 1899. John B. Rae describes that version of the legend in his book *The American Automobile: A Brief History* (1965). According to the story, Packard bought one of the first Winton cars and went to the factory in Cleveland to complain about certain faults. Instead of accepting Packard's criticisms, Winton told him to make his own car if he didn't like the one he'd bought. In the legend, that sparked Packard's entry into the car business.

★ ★ A plastic model of the U.S.S. *Nautilus* submarine was recalled from hobby shops because it was so detailed and accurate that the Russians might have used it as a source of classified information. (1961)

Almost true. In June 1961, Vice Admiral Hyman Rickover complained about the accuracy of certain model kits, claiming that they could save the Russians millions of dollars in espionage. He singled out a plastic model of a Polaris-launching submarine, made by the Revell toy company, as one of the worst offenders. Revell's model could be opened to reveal a detailed plan of the inside of the sub, including the power plant, living quarters, and even the launching tubes for the missiles. Inside the launching tubes were spring-powered scale models of the Polaris missiles. But though the model bothered Admiral Rickover, and his complaint received wide publicity, the toy was never recalled.

Rickover was undoubtedly right in his claim that the plastic models could be valuable sources of technical information for our enemies. Revell went to great lengths to ferret out design specifications and plans for the latest military ships and aircraft, and their models were often available in stores very soon after the full-scale hardware was unveiled. American missile companies used the models to show technicians how the real components were assembled, and the armed forces often used the toys for training demonstrations and reduced-scale tests. If the models were so useful to the Americans, they must also have been of great interest to the Russians.

In defense of the toy company, however, we must point out that Revell's models were based on public information. The company's researchers worked from published photographs and plans that were available to anyone and from declassified blueprints of the various components of the vessel. No secret plans were used in creating the models. In reply to Admiral Rickover's charge, Revell's president said, "We wouldn't touch classified material with a ten-foot pole."

Twenty-five years later another plastic model drew fire for its alleged exposure of military secrets. In the spring of 1986, Testor Corp., of Rockford, Illinois, brought out a model of the F-19, or Stealth, fighter, an aircraft so secret that the Pentagon won't even admit that it exists. Because no photographs of the plane have been released to the public, the model's designer had to rely on other sources of information to find out what the aircraft looked like. One lead came from a commercial pilot who saw one of the planes near an air force test site in Nevada. A model fan, he sent a sketch of the fighter to Testor.

Because the Stealth project is so secret, the model company has been spared the open fury of the Pentagon. When asked to cómment on the model before a House panel, Donald Hicks, Undersecretary of Defense for Research and Engineering, said, "My comment is that there is no F-19 program. It does not exist."

★ ★ In the area of ocean known as the Bermuda Triangle, an abnormally high number of ships and planes have mysteriously disappeared or been abandoned, often in calm, sunny weather. There is no earthly explanation for these tragedies. (1950s)

Not true. Over the past thirty-five years, a popular myth has grown up around the so-called Bermuda Triangle, the area bounded by Bermuda, Cuba, and Puerto Rico. Books have been written and movies made about the mystery, and some of the writers and filmmakers have made a great deal of money from the myth. To heighten the drama of their stories, writers have given sensational names to the region: Limbo of the Lost, the Devil's Triangle, the Hoodoo Sea, the Twilight Zone, and the Port of Missing Ships. But very rarely have these writers weighed the evidence piece by piece to determine if anything unusual has really happened. Many of the mysteries attributed to the Bermuda Triangle can be explained by bad weather or inexperience; some of the most dramatic losses at sea have occurred outside the region—in the Gulf of Mexico, the North Atlantic, or even the Pacific Ocean.

Lawrence David Kusche refutes the legend of the Bermuda Triangle, incident by incident, in his book *The Bermuda Triangle Mystery Solved* (1975). Unlike many of the writers who have sensationalized the legend, Kusche did some careful research. He checked newspaper records for sailing dates of the missing ships and for firsthand accounts of discoveries, checked weather reports for storms, looked at maps to see where disappearances occurred, and read the accident investigation reports prepared by the navy, the Coast Guard, the Civil Aeronautics Board, and Lloyds of London. We don't have room to recount all the incidents connected with the Bermuda Triangle legend, but we'll give a few examples to show how the myth measures up to the truth that Kusche uncovered.

On December 4, 1872, the *Mary Celeste*, a 103-foot-long brigantine, was found drifting abandoned between the Azores and Portugal. The sails were set and the boat looked to be in good condition. The only clue to the whereabouts of the passengers and crew was the missing lifeboat. Some accounts of the discovery add to the mystery with such details as warm food found on the table and a bloody sword found in the captain's bedroom, but these are almost certainly fictitious embellishments. No survivors from the *Mary Celeste* were ever found, and the fate of those on board remains one of the great unsolved puzzles of the sea. However, it is hardly accurate to include the *Mary Celeste*, as some writers have done, in the list of victims of the Bermuda Triangle. The ship was found on the far side of the Atlantic, thousands of miles from the borders of the "mystery" region.

The U.S.S. *Cyclops*, a 542-foot navy supply ship, did disappear within the limits of the Bermuda Triangle in early March 1918, while carrying a load of coal from Barbados to Norfolk. It was one of the largest ships on the ocean at the time and became one of the first radio-equipped vessels to disappear without broadcasting a distress signal. According to the Bermuda Triangle legend, no bad weather was reported along the ship's route, and the navy remains puzzled to this day as to why no debris from the ship was ever found. At first, speculation about the loss centered on German sabotage or submarine attack. But, after the war, a search of German records showed that no submarines had been operating in the area of the ship's course during the first part of March, and the Germans had not captured or sabotaged the boat. Like most of the Bermuda Triangle losses, the disappearance of the *Cyclops* draws much of its mystery from the fine weather in which the accident is said to have occurred. In fact, a powerful storm hit the east coast of the United States on March 9 and 10, just as the boat was scheduled to arrive in Norfolk. Winds of eighty-four miles an hour were measured in New York City, and gale warnings were issued south along the coast to Florida. Such a storm might easily have sunk the *Cyclops*. In 1968 a navy diver discovered an unusual wreck seventy miles east of Norfolk, lying in one hundred eighty feet of water. The diver was struck by the curious design of the ship, its high bridge propped on stilts, and the ring of tall, upright beams that surrounded the deck. When he later saw a photograph of the *Cyclops*, he was sure that it was the boat he had found. Unfortunately, attempts to relocate the wreck have not been successful. While the fate of the *Cyclops* is not certain, the overlooked storm does make it far less of a mystery.

The disappearance of five navy training planes, Flight 19, on December 5, 1945, features prominently in most accounts of the Bermuda Triangle mystery and has even been the subject of a movie. According to the legend, the pilots of Flight 19 were experienced flyers traveling over familiar territory in good weather. The planes took off from Fort Lauderdale, Florida, in the early afternoon and vanished into thin air somewhere near the Bahamas a few hours later. A rescue plane sent out to find them met the same curious fate. The facts, as revealed in the navy's inquiry into the loss, are not quite so mysterious: only the leader of the group could be considered an experienced pilot, while the men in the other planes were students in training. The group got into trouble when the lead plane's compasses malfunctioned and the pilot became disoriented. At the time the flight was directly on course, flying north over Grand Bahama Island, but in his confusion, the flight leader decided they were over the Florida Keys and altered the course accordingly. If the group had flown west, they would have reached the Florida coast. Instead they flew north into the open Atlantic Ocean. By the time radio monitors in Florida could establish the flight's position, the flyers were so far off course that it was impossible to send them instructions. When the first plane ran out of gas, all five followed it down into the ocean on the instructions of the flight leader. Though the weather had been clear when the flight took off, by the time the planes went down, strong winds had picked up and the sea was extremely rough. One of several planes sent out to locate the flight did disappear as mentioned in the legend, but the crash was caused by a fuel explosion, witnessed from a nearby ship.

Many disappearances at sea can never be fully explained because the evidence is swallowed by the ocean, but these losses occur in oceans all over the world, and it is misleading to assign greater weight to those that occur in the Bermuda Triangle. Taken one by one, the mysteries of the Bermuda Triangle can be reduced to the simple tragedies that they really are.

★★ The U.S. Navy conducted experiments in teletransportation during World War II. In the most dramatic of these tests, an entire warship was rendered invisible and transported from Philadelphia to Norfolk and back in a few minutes. Many of the crew members died or went crazy, and the system was abandoned as impractical. (1950s)

Unconfirmed. The legendary warship test has been dubbed the "Philadelphia Experiment" by believers, and in both dramatic detail and lack of factual evidence it matches stories of UFO landings and Bermuda Triangle disappearances. Morris Jessup printed the first sketchy account of the test in his 1956 book *The Case for UFOs* and soon afterward began receiving letters from a man named Carlos Allende, who claimed to have witnessed the experiment. The rambling and almost incoherent letters suggest that the writer was not in full possession of his faculties, yet the notes are relied on by believers as real evidence that the experiment took place.

In his first letter, Allende claimed that the work in teletransportation was based on Albert Einstein's unified field theory:

The 'result' was complete invisibility of a ship, Destroyer type, *and all* of its crew While at Sea. (Oct. 1943) The Field Was effective in an oblate spheroidal shape, extending one hundred yards (More or Less, due to Lunar position & Latitude) *out* from each beam of the ship. Any Person Within that sphere became vague in form BUT He too observed Persons aboard *that* ship as though they too were of the same state, yet were walking upon nothing....There are only a very few of the original Experimental D-E's Crew Left by Now, Sir. Most went insane, one just walked 'throo' His quarters Wall in sight of His Wife & Child & 2 other crew Members (WAS NEVER SEEN AGAIN), two Went into 'The Flame,' I.E. They 'Froze' & caught fire, while carrying common Small-Boat Compasses, one Man carried the compass & Caught fire, the other came for the 'Laying on of Hands' as he was the nearest but he too, took fire. THEY BURNED FOR 18 DAYS. The faith in 'Hand Laying' Died When this Happened & Mens Minds Went by the scores. The experiment Was a Complete Success. The Men Were Complete Failures.

Allende went on to tell Jessup to check the Philadelphia newspapers "for a tiny Paragraph (upper Half of sheet, inside the paper Near the

3rd of Paper, 1944-46 in Spring or Fall or Winter, NOT Summer)" that described a barroom disturbance caused by the sailors when they returned to shore from the experimental voyage. He also suggested that clues might be found in the log of the S.S. *Andrew Furuseth* for the fall of 1943.

Jessup died in 1959, but others have tried to pick up the trail and find out if there is any truth to Allende's allegations. William Moore and Charles Berlitz, in their 1979 book *The Philadelphia Experiment: Project Invisibility*, turned up a little more information, but hardly enough to support their conviction that the experiment really did happen. They found an able seaman certificate issued to a man named Carl Allen in March 1944, and concluded that this is the Carlos Allende who later wrote to Jessup. Surviving records show that Allen sailed on the Matson Navigation Company's S.S. *Furuseth* on two voyages in the fall of 1943, both from Virginia to North Africa and back. As Allende-Allen did not claim to have been aboard the experimental vessel, Moore and Berlitz had to find another boat that crossed paths with the *Furuseth* in the fall of 1943 and disappeared for a few minutes. Here the authors had more trouble. Relying on some research and some bold assumptions, they named the U.S.S. *Eldridge*, but could only put it in Philadelphia with Allen by disregarding the ship's official record. Their solution requires the *Eldridge* to have disappeared sometime between its launch in Newark, New Jersey, on July 25 and its commissioning in New York on August 27. As the

Furuseth did not travel to Philadelphia during that time, they conclude that Allen must have gone there on his own and seen the newspaper account on August 14 or 15.

Though Moore and Berlitz rely on Allende's letters as the principal evidence of the ship's disappearance, they make light of the discrepancies between the information in the letters and that contained in the factual records. Allende's first letter dates the experiment in October 1943, yet Moore and Berlitz decide it must have taken place in July or August. Allende was also sure that he did not see the newspaper article in the summer, yet the authors pinpoint it in mid-August. At first glance, the Allende letters seem like an unreliable source of information about a technical project, which, if actually carried out, must have involved scores of scientists and other witnesses. On further investigation, the letters seem even less believable.

The navy's official position on the legendary experiment is fairly straightforward. Inquiries are answered with a firm denial: "The Office of Naval Research has never conducted any investigations on invisibility, either in 1943 or at any other time. In view of present scientific knowledge, our scientists do not believe that such an experiment could be possible except in the realm of science fiction. A scientific discovery of such import, if it had in fact occurred, could hardly remain secret for such a long time."

★ ★ A human clone has been created in the laboratory. A wealthy American businessman paid a million dollars to fund a secret research project that resulted in his own genetic duplication. (1978)

Unconfirmed. This is more of a hoax than a rumor, as its source is a single published account. David Rorvick, in his book *In His Image: The Cloning of a Man,* claims to describe actual events that led to the cloning of an unnamed businessman in 1977. According to Rorvick, he was unable to disclose names, places, and specific details of the cloning because the "father" wanted to protect the privacy of the child and because the scientists worried that knowledge of their involvement might damage their professional reputations. According to Rorvick's critics, he did not print the details necessary to verify the experiment because it had never occurred.

Rorvick has consistently maintained that the cloning did take place and that the child is growing up happily. Most scientists, however, doubt that human cloning was possible at the time of Rorvick's book. Almost twenty years ago, frogs were successfully cloned by replacing the nucleus of an egg with the nucleus of a cell from the body of another frog. But mammal eggs are far smaller than frog eggs—roughly a thousand times smaller—and the surgical techniques necessary to repeat the cloning on a mammal had not been perfected in 1977. After the book came out, however, one researcher managed to clone mice in the laboratory (though the results have not been confirmed by independent researchers using the same techniques), and Rorvick's scenario no longer seems quite so farfetched. The routine creation of test-tube babies since 1978 has also shown that if a cloned egg could be created, it would be a relatively straightforward matter to culture it and implant it in a woman's womb.

★★ NASA scientists have discovered a "lost" day in their computer models of the earth's orbital history. The missing time coincides with the biblical account of Joshua commanding the sun and moon to stand still. (1960s)

Not true. In the late 1950s and early 1960s, NASA did do computer studies of the earth's orbit and the movement of other planets in order to determine optimum rocket launching times and trajectories. But space agency scientists never delved into studies of earth time history, and they did not prove the existence of Joshua's "lost" day. Any calendar study that reached back thousands of years would be well beyond the scope of NASA's interest in planetary movements and would become mired in the conflicting calendar systems followed by different cultures through the centuries.

According to Terry White, a NASA spokesman who has fielded questions about the rumor for years, the story began to pester the agency in the early 1960s. Inspirational pamphlets, newspaper articles, letters to the editor, and radio stories have periodically picked the story up and helped it along. These reports often name the scientists who reputedly made the discovery and add convincing details about how the find was made. Attempts to verify the story by contacting the people and companies mentioned in the reports have proved fruitless and reveal only that these "facts" are further embellishments on the rumor.

One pamphlet, "The Missing Day in Time," by Harry L. Miller, gives a typically detailed account of the discovery, placing the research at the Goddard Space Flight Center in Green Belt, Maryland. According to the pamphlet, scientists

were using a computer to check the positions of the sun, moon and planets over centuries and millennia. As they ran the computer measurement back and forth it came to a halt and put up a red signal. Something was wrong with the information fed into it or with the results as compared to the standards. The head of operations said, "We've found there is a day missing in space in elapsed time."

The space scientists were baffled until one of the team members said, "I remember in Sunday School the talk about the sun standing still."

He brought in a Bible and quoted from *Joshua*, Chapter 10: "Then spake Joshua to the Lord in the day when the Lord delivered up the Amorites before the children of Israel, and he said in the sight of Israel, Sun stand thou still upon Gibeon; and thou, Moon, in the valley of Ajàlon. And the sun stood still, and the moon stayed, until the people had avenged

45

themselves upon their enemies. So the sun stood still in the midst of heaven and hastened not to go down about a whole day."

The pamphlet goes on to claim that the scientists thought they'd solved the problem, but a further check back into the planetary records at the time of Joshua showed that they'd only found a missing twenty-three hours and twenty minutes. They were still forty minutes off.

The team checked the Bible again and found in *II Kings*, Chapter 20: "And Hezekiah said unto Isaiah, what shall be the sign that the Lord will heal me and that I shall go up into the house of the Lord the third day? And Isaiah said, this sign shalt thou have of the Lord, that the Lord will do the thing he has spoken: shall the shadow go forward ten degrees or back ten degrees? And Hezekiah answered, it is a light thing for the shadow to go down ten degrees: nay, but let the shadow return backward ten degrees. And Isaiah the prophet cried unto the Lord and he brought the shadow ten degrees backward, by which it had gone down on the dial of Ahaz."

Ten degrees is forty minutes. The missing day in the universe had been found.

Essentially the same account is given each time the story is retold or reprinted, and this pamphlet or one very similar to it may well be at the root of all the versions. We checked with the Goddard Space Flight Center and were politely told that no "missing" day has ever been discovered at the facility.

★ ★ Abraham Lincoln's voice was recorded on an early sound-recording machine, but the only copy of the historic pressing has been lost. (1950s)

Not true. Thomas Edison built the first successful sound-recording device in 1877, twelve years after Lincoln's death. The first voice recorded on this phonograph was Edison's, reciting "Mary Had a Little Lamb." The voices of a few other nineteenth-century luminaries have survived on early phonographs, among them P. T. Barnum, William Gladstone, and Alfred, Lord Tennyson.

Wishful thinking is probably at the root of the story about Lincoln's voice. Even though the recording is lost in the rumor, at least it wasn't destroyed, and its future discovery is still an enticing possibility. Similar stories about other lost treasures often leave open the hope that the missing item could still turn up. One rumor tells of a master tape for an unreleased Beatles album that was burned in a fire and never rerecorded. But according to the story, a pirated copy had been made just days earlier. The owners of the illegal tape have been holding on to it for twenty years, afraid that they'll be caught if they try to sell copies. Again, the story seems to hold out the hope that the music may yet be heard. A more pessimistic rumor holds that a longer version of the film *Citizen Kane* was destroyed in a fire at Orson Welles's home. No pirates to the rescue in this story; the ultimate version of the classic film is simply gone forever.

A few early recordings really have disappeared, and these lost treasures may be the inspiration for the story of the lost Lincoln disk. Hans von Bülow, the famous German pianist, visited Edison's laboratories in 1888 and recorded a passage from a Chopin piece onto an experimental cylinder. That recording may have been the only one von Bülow ever made, and it has vanished without a trace.

★ ★ The Vatican is concealing evidence that can prove or disprove the historical existence of Jesus Christ.

Unconfirmed. The Vatican, a tiny city-state of just over a hundred acres, embodies much of the wonder and mystery of the Christian faith, with a healthy measure of bureaucratic secrecy. But, despite the official veil that cloaks much of the church's activities there, it seems unlikely that proof of the actual existence of Jesus Christ could be concealed for centuries—or that it would be. Pieces of the cross, bones of saints, and other holy relics have long served the church in a positive way, as items of interest and points of focus for the faithful. Any true record or relic of Jesus

Christ would provide an enormous popular draw for the church.

As for the other side of the rumor, we have trouble imagining what sort of evidence might be used to disprove the existence of Christ. Our own researches have shown that it is virtually impossible to prove a negative—to show beyond doubt, for example, that the U.S. Air Force does *not* hold captured UFOs. It is conceivable that the church has evidence that might lead some to question Christ's existence and that such information is being held back in the natural self-interest of an organization built on Christ's teachings.

The rumor may have something to do with the centuries-old legend that St. Peter's Basilica, the huge church that dominates the Vatican City, is built over the grave of St. Peter. Catholic tradition holds that Simon Peter, to whom Christ passed the leadership of the church at his death, was himself crucified upside down in about 65 A.D. and buried in a Roman graveyard. Emperor Constantine built the first church on Vatican Hill on the site of that graveyard some three hundred years later. The current basilica was built over Constantine's church, and was consecrated in 1626.

The story of St. Peter's grave remained in the realm of legend until the middle of this century. In 1939, when Pope Pius XI died, his successor ordered excavations in the grottoes beneath the basilica to make room for the dead pope's tomb. As soon as the workers began to dig among the tombs of past popes, they discovered an ancient burial ground on a lower level. Over the next ten years, the church conducted a thorough, and secret, archaeological study of the ground beneath the basilica. They discovered that the present basilica had been aligned almost exactly with Constantine's early structure, with the high altar positioned just above the location of the earlier altar. Directly beneath they found an early Christian shrine, from the second century A.D., built over a grave. The grave was empty, but a set of bones nearby proved to be those of a large man who had died at about the age of sixty-five. A creative reading of graffiti found on walls around the shrine, and the neat match of the bones to the image of Peter described in the Bible convinced many that the grave and shrine belonged to the saint. In 1968 Pope Paul VI pronounced the bones Peter's and had them placed in the empty grave.

★ ★ A film about the sex life of Jesus Christ is currently in production in a large midwestern city. (1984)

Not true. Since the mid-1970s people have been agitated by this persistent rumor, and their concern has brought floods of protest letters to those reputed to be responsible for the film. During 1984, the office of the Illinois attorney general received more than 180,000 letters of complaint asking that legal steps be taken to halt the production. Unfortunately, neither the attorney general nor the letter-writing public has been able to track down the mysterious film crew.

Christian Century magazine brought the story to the public's attention in 1975 when it reported that the Danish Film Institute had voted to fund a film titled *The Many Faces of Jesus*, which was to be produced by Jens Jorgen Thorsen, who planned to "show Jesus in several nude and love-making scenes." According to the magazine, after the funding was approved, the dissenting board members resigned in protest, while those who had approved the grant resigned to protect the producer from political recriminations. That bizarre logic set off our rumor sensors immediately, but the magazine, with its indignation aroused, suggested that readers "would not be remiss in protesting this depiction of their Lord as a fornicator and in praying that God will show them how to make their protest most effectively." We have been unable to turn up any other information about the Thorsen film, and we suspect its production was a rumor from the start. If the film really was planned in 1975, it has yet to be released.

A Chicago-based tabloid called *Modern People News* published the story of the allegedly planned sex film in 1976 and unwittingly provided a target for the outrage of the faithful. For some reason the public decided that the tabloid was connected with the film's production, and people began to write and call the paper to protest. By 1980 the rumor had grown even more provocative, asserting that the film was being made right in Chicago and that it portrayed Jesus as a homosexual. To word of mouth were added the powerful rumor-spreading devices of the mimeograph and photocopy machines. *Modern People News* received thousands of letters each week, many of them form letters clipped or copied from a widely circulated mimeographed sheet outlining the story.

In 1983, the rumor's fury was redirected at Paramount Pictures, which had contracted with Martin Scorsese for a film version of Nikos Kazantzakis's novel *The Last Temptation of Christ*. The book's title was unfortunate, given the mood created by the rumor, but the story merely depicts the human side of a Christ who didn't want to become the Messiah. It is a controversial theme, but not pornographic. After being swamped with letters of protest, Paramount decided to drop the project just a month before filming was to begin.

Since then, the letter writers have focused their attention on the law-enforcement agencies of the various states in which the film is rumored to be in production. The attorney general of Illinois has received the bulk of the complaints, and his office has mounted a "determined" national campaign to quell the rumor, soliciting the aid of church leaders and syndicated columnists. As of this writing, the story shows no sign of abating.

★ ★ The FCC is planning to ban all religious radio and television programming. (1975)

Not true. The Federal Communications Commission has never considered banning religious programming. By law the FCC is prohibited from censoring broadcast material, and, under the First Amendment of the Constitution, it is required to maintain a neutral stance toward religion.

The rumor began in 1975, soon after the FCC received a petition from Jeremy D. Lansman and Lorenzo W. Milam asking the agency to look into the practices of noncommercial educational broadcasters. The petition asked the agency to hold up all applications by religious groups for the use of channels reserved for educational broadcast until the inquiry had been completed. The FCC turned down the petition, citing the First Amendment's guarantees to freedom of speech and free exercise of religion.

Apparently an alarm about the Lansman-Milam petition went out in certain religious circles and the petition's scope was vastly exaggerated in the bustle of concern. The FCC began receiving letters and phone calls from people who thought the agency was favorably considering a petition to ban all religious programming from radio and television. Some of these callers and writers thought that Madalyn Murray O'Hair, the well-known atheist, was the sponsor of the petition and that she had been granted a hearing on the matter. This elaboration has become the most common version of the story and is the rumor that has plagued the FCC now for more than a decade. (In fact, O'Hair never had anything to do with the Lansman-Milam petition, has never filed a similar petition, and has no intention of doing so. She is privately flattered by the importance the rumor grants her.)

Since those first calls and letters began coming in during the early months of 1975, the FCC has patiently explained the truth of the matter to each and every caller and letter writer. In 1982 the stream of protests reached flood proportions; during that year and the next letters came in at a rate of more than one hundred thirty thousand a month. The FCC estimates that by the end of 1985 it had received more than sixteen million letters about the rumor, and at least as many phone calls. That kind of concern is only good for the telephone companies.

★★ Six Chicago high school students built a copy of the ark of the covenant, following the description given in the Bible. They had to destroy it when it became too powerful. (1970)

Unconfirmed. This is one of those wonderful and mysterious rumors that leaves the listener wanting to know more. Are there really instructions in the Bible for building a force machine? If a group of high school students could build such a thing, wouldn't it be an easy job for experts to build another? And just what do they mean by "too powerful"?

The original ark of the covenant was built by Moses following the instructions of God in Exodus 25:10; the ark was a box to hold the stone tablets on which God carved the ten commandments, his covenant with the people of Israel. God gave the instructions for the ark in a long speech that also included elaborate plans for a table, a lampstand, and a tentlike tabernacle.

The story of the students' copy probably grew out of a suggestion made by Erich von Däniken in his book *Chariots of the Gods*. He proposed the idea that the ark was actually a powerful battery and that God may have been a creature from another planet who told Moses to build the ark as a means of communication between Earth and the spaceship. That's a pretty wild idea, and it is based on some shaky assumptions. Däniken refers to a later mention of the ark in 2 Samuel 6, where Uzzah grabbed the ark to keep it from falling off a cart. Angered because he had touched the ark, God struck Uzzah dead, "and he died there beside the ark of God." Däniken takes that passage as proof that the ark was electrically charged. He claims that, "if we reconstruct it according to the instructions handed down by Moses, an electrical conductor of several hundred volts is produced."

Perhaps Däniken and those students in Chicago had access to a longer and more elaborate version of the Bible than we have seen. Here is God's instruction to Moses as written in Exodus 25:

They shall make an ark of acacia wood; two cubits and a half shall be its length, a cubit and a half its breadth, and a cubit and a half its height. And you shall overlay it with pure gold, within and without shall you overlay it, and you shall make upon it a molding of gold round about. And you shall cast four rings of gold for it and put them on its four feet, two rings on the one side of it, and two rings on the other side of it. You shall make poles of acacia wood, and overlay them with gold. And you shall put the poles into the rings on the side of the ark, to carry the ark by them. The poles shall remain in the rings of the ark; they shall not be taken from it. And you shall put into the ark the testimony which I shall give you.

We haven't tried to build an ark, as we don't have access to that much gold and acacia wood, but it doesn't seem like much of a battery to us. Moses may not have left a complete set of instructions behind, however, because his ark did behave a little strangely. When he put God's tablets in the ark and set it in its place in the tabernacle, a cloud filled the tent and Moses was not able to enter. According to Exodus 40, "throughout all their journeys the cloud of the Lord was upon the tabernacle by day, and fire was in it by night."

It seems as though the key to the power of the ark lay in the tablets given to Moses by God. Perhaps those Chicago high school students figured out the secret of the tablets. Or maybe they uncovered a better set of plans.

★ ★ *The Exorcist* was based on a real exorcism performed at Alexian Brothers Hospital in St. Louis. Afterward the room in which the exorcism had been performed was permanently sealed and has never been reopened. (1974)

Partly true. William Peter Blatty's novel

The Exorcist and the film made from the book were based on an actual exorcism performed in 1949 and widely reported in the press. The victim of that apparently genuine possession was a fourteen-year-old boy from Mt. Rainier, Maryland (it was a girl in the book and movie). The boy's troubles began in November 1948, soon after the death of an aunt who had believed in spirits and who had taught him how to use a Ouija board. According to press reports published at the time, the boy and his parents heard scratching noises under the floor of his bedroom, and rodent poison put beneath the floor did nothing to stop the sounds. The boy's clothes began to move overnight from the chair beside his bed to other places in the house. Objects in the house began to levitate and fly around. When the boy was in bed, his mattress sometimes floated into the air. Worried by these bizarre occurrences, his parents called on their Lutheran minister, who offered to take the boy into his own home. When the levitations continued there, the minister sought help from a Catholic priest. The parents agreed to let that church try an exorcism.

Local hospitals refused to allow a room of theirs to be used for the exorcism, and, when it was attempted at the family's home, reports began to appear in local papers. So the boy was taken to St. Louis, where the Alexian Brothers Hospital agreed to admit him. A Jesuit priest was assigned to be the exorcist. During the day the boy acted quite normally, but at night he was transformed completely. The levitations continued, and the child's features would be grotesquely distorted, while he swore in a gravelly voice and spat in the exorcist's face. By night the boy showed a good working knowledge of Latin. At the height of the exorcism, red "brandings" appeared on his body in the form of words and symbols. These were sometimes severe enough to bleed.

In early April, the boy's disturbances suddenly ended. He woke up from a nap and described a dream in which a white-clad Roman soldier had drawn a flaming sword and used it to drive a pack of snarling demons into a deep pit. That afternoon, people all over the hospital heard a loud bang "like a gunshot" come from the boy's room. From that moment he was cured. His identity has been closely guarded by all connected with the exorcism, and he now lives a normal life.

Those are the facts as gathered from press reports at the time and from later interviews with those connected with the exorcism. It is not true that the room in which the boy stayed at the Alexian Brothers Hospital was later sealed and has never been reopened. A spokesman for the hospital says that the room remained open, but that the wing in which it stood has since been

torn down. A similar rumor, also untrue, places
the sealed room in DuBorg Hall at St. Louis University.

★ ★ Pope John Paul I was murdered. (1978)

Possibly true. Pope John Paul I was found
dead in his Vatican bed on the morning of September 29, 1978, just thirty-three days after he
assumed the papacy. No autopsy was performed,
yet Vatican doctors confidently announced that
the pope had died of a heart attack. To back up
this verdict, church officials pointed to John
Paul's allegedly frail health.

Others were not so sure. Family members
noted that neither the pope nor any of his close
relatives had had a history of heart trouble. His
previous medical problems had included a child-
hood bout with pneumonia and operations for the
removal of tonsils, adenoids, gallstones, and hem-
orrhoids. In 1975 he had suffered from a blood
clot in his left eye, but this had been cleared
up without an operation. A July 1978 health
checkup had included an EKG, a test designed to
reveal heart disease, and it had shown nothing
out of the ordinary. The pope's blood pressure was
low, another indication that he was not a likely
candidate for heart trouble.

Because no autopsy was performed, and because the body was embalmed just fourteen hours after it was found, many wondered whether the Vatican was covering up something. Rumors of foul play began to fly. Minor conflicts in the official reports of the death were pounced on as evidence of a sinister plot. The first report announced that the pope had been found at 5:30 A.M. by the Reverend John Magee and that the pontiff had been holding a copy of *The Imitation of Christ*, a fifteenth-century devotional essay. When it later came out that a nun, Sister Vincenza, had first found the body at 4:45 A.M., and that the pope had been reading some personal papers when he died, many assumed that the first reports had been concocted to conceal something. What notes had John Paul been reading that the Vatican did not want the world to know about? And why was Sister Vincenza's role in the discovery being covered up? What had she seen?

David Yallop, in his book *In God's Name: An Investigation into the Murder of Pope John Paul I*, explores these questions and raises many others in presenting his own opinion that Pope John Paul I was murdered. While Yallop does not present hard evidence of murder, he does amass a great volume of circumstantial evidence that suggests that many people had motives for murder. The pope favored an end to the church's ban on artificial birth control, and Yallop speculates that conservative elements within the church may have felt sufficiently threatened by his position to want the new pope dead. More convincing is Yallop's theory that the murder was related to the financial dealings of the Vatican Bank. As the Vatican is a sovereign state, its financial transactions have largely been shielded from outside investigation, but the actions of its trading partners have brought some true scandal to light.

In the 1960s and 70s, the Vatican Bank did a great deal of business with two Italian financiers who were later revealed to be less than honest businessmen. Michele Sindona advised the Vatican on financial matters until 1974, when the collapse of the Franklin National Bank began to bring to light the extent of his illegal maneuvers. Sindona had purchased the Franklin National Bank in 1972 with an illegal transfer of money from an Italian bank he controlled; its collapse was the largest bank failure in U.S. history, and it cost the Vatican Bank an estimated $50 million. In the ensuing investigations, Sindona was revealed to be involved with both the Mafia and a shadowy Masonic lodge known as P-2 that had far-reaching connections in Italian government and in organized crime. In 1986, Sindona was sentenced to life imprisonment for arranging the 1979 contract killing of an Italian investigator who was looking into the fraudulent dealings of his companies. Four days after his conviction, Sindona died of cyanide poisoning.

After Sindona's fall from grace in 1974, the Vatican Bank stepped up its dealings with Roberto Calvi, an associate of Sindona's and a member of P-2. According to Yallop, the Vatican had been engaged in suspect stock transactions with Calvi since the early 1970s, but, after 1974, these increased. Yallop describes how the Vatican

Bank, in conjunction with Calvi's Banco Ambrosiano, became involved in the creation of shell corporations in Latin America and other fraudulent transactions that earned a high rate of return for both institutions. In the spring of 1982, an investigation into Banco Ambrosiano's assets revealed that the bank had lost $790 million in fraudulent loans to Latin American companies that existed only on paper. At the same time, Calvi became a target of an Italian government investigation into the operations of P-2. On June 19, the financier was found hanging from London's Blackfriars Bridge. It is not known whether his death was murder or suicide.

At the time of Pope John Paul I's death, the Vatican Bank does seem to have been engaged in some less than saintly business transactions. It is possible that the new pope intended to clean up the bank's operations and that Calvi, Sindona, their associates in P-2 or officials at the Vatican Bank felt that the resulting risk of exposure would be too great to bear. Sindona demonstrated in 1979 that he knew how to arrange a murder, and it is likely that Calvi had similar connections. But whether either man actually went so far as to arrange the murder of the pope remains a matter of speculation. And, since both are now dead, the truth may never be fully revealed.

★ ★ George Reeves, the star of the television series *Superman* in the 1950s, died in a fall from a skyscraper when he attempted to fly. He had become so involved in his television role that he thought he really *was* Superman. (1960)

Not true. George Reeves died under mysterious circumstances, but his death did not result from an attempted Superman flight. At 2:30 on the morning of June 16, 1959, Reeves, his fiancée,

Lenore Lemmon, and another guest at his Hollywood home were awakened by the visit of two friends, William Bliss and Carol Van Ronkel. Reeves argued with Bliss about the lateness of the visit, then apologized and returned to his bedroom. According to an Associated Press report published the next day, Lemmon made a bizarre prediction of the actor's suicide. "He's going to shoot himself," she said. The others laughed it off, but she continued. "He's opening a drawer to get the gun." Then the sound of a gunshot came from the bedroom. "See there—I told you," she blurted. They found Reeves lying dead on his bed with a bullet wound in his head.

Friends of the actor said he had been depressed over his inability to find another film or television role. Reeves had played supporting parts in many films, including *Gone With the Wind* and *From Here to Eternity*, but after 1951 he was best known for his work as Superman.

Another persistent rumor claims that Reeves was shot by his housekeeper. Police ruled the death a suicide, but the actor's mother hired a private investigator to look into the possibility of murder, and her doubts in all likelihood sparked this second rumor.

★ ★ Bruce Lee was murdered by a Kung Fu master because he had revealed martial arts secrets to the public. (1973)

Unconfirmed. Bruce Lee died on the night of July 20, 1973, after falling into a coma at the apartment of a young Hong Kong actress. Lee's producer at first told the press that he had discovered the actor unconscious on his own bed, but when that lie was exposed by an ambulance official, rumors of more shocking secrets grew rampant in Hong Kong and eventually spread through the rest of the world. Adding fuel to the rumors was Lee's apparent good health at the time of his death. He was only thirty-two years old, and his film image as one of the fittest men in the world made it hard for many to believe he could have died a natural death.

In fact, Lee had suffered a similar coma just a month earlier, and doctors in Los Angeles judged it to have been a sort of epileptic convulsion. They could not tell what had caused the collapse, but they prescribed a drug called Dilantin, which is used by many epileptics. Lee was a fanatic about his health and training, and his diet and exercise regimen may have contributed to his death. He trained for hours every day and ate mostly raw beef, eggs, milk, and fruit and vegetable juices. He also had the sweat glands removed from his armpits in order to improve his appearance on film. In the months before his death his weight fell from 140 to 120 pounds, and the weight loss may have been a signal of more serious trouble.

On the day of his death, Lee spent the afternoon with his producer, Raymond Chow, at the home of actress Betty Ting Pei. Chow later testified that they were there to talk the actress into co-starring in Lee's next film. Lee complained of a headache, and Betty Ting gave him a pill for it, a prescription painkiller called Equagesic. Chow left while Lee went into the actress's bedroom to rest. She later tried to wake him, and, when he wouldn't respond, she called Chow and her doctor. Lee was taken by ambulance to Queen Elizabeth Hospital, where he died at 11:30 P.M. An autopsy revealed that his brain had swollen dramatically, probably in an allergic reaction to the Equagesic pill, and that the resulting seizure had killed him.

The first rumors about Lee's death concerned his presence in Betty Ting's bedroom, which had not been admitted in the earliest announcements of the death. The rumors told of affairs with numerous actresses and blamed the death on "too much sex." Some whispered that the death had been caused by Spanish Fly, a supposed aphrodisiac that can in fact be dangerous. Doctors performing the autopsy were aware of this rumor, but their search of Lee's body turned up no trace of the substance.

After a funeral in Hong Kong, Lee's remains were flown to Seattle for burial. His expensive bronze casket was damaged during the flight and had to be replaced in Seattle. That switch sparked rumors that Lee was still alive—that he "woke up" on the flight and went into hiding somewhere in the United States. According to this rumor, another body was stolen from the Seattle morgue to fill Lee's coffin at the funeral.

As the rumors spread from Hong Kong they grew stranger and more sinister. Some said the Mafia had killed Lee "because he was getting too big." Others said that a servant had poisoned him or that he had been killed by a rival Kung Fu master either out of jealousy or from fear that he might reveal important secrets of the martial art. Ben Block, in his book *The Legend of Bruce Lee*, tops even the wildest rumors with speculation that the actor was killed by "the art of the vibrating palm," a secret killing technique that does the victim in by converting internal energy into vibrations. According to Block, the fatal touch could have been administered months or even years before it finally struck Lee down.

In the face of these bizarre stories we can only point to the official autopsy report, which was based on a careful examination of Lee's body. Bruce Lee was not murdered at all, but died from his body's reaction to a pill he took for a headache.

★ ★ Adelle Davis, the famous nutritionist, died of stomach cancer. (1974)

Not true. Adelle Davis spent her life advocating healthier eating habits, at first as a nutritionist for hospitals, schools, and health clinics,

and later as a best-selling author. Her books—
*Let's Eat Right to Keep Fit, Let's Cook It Right,
Let's Get Well,* and *Let's Have Healthy Children*—
brought her message to millions. In 1973 she was
diagnosed as having bone cancer. She reacted to
the news with shock and self-criticism. After
years of telling others that they could avoid disease and early death by keeping to a sound diet,
she now unfairly blamed herself for having contracted cancer. She told one interviewer, "I
thought this was for people who drink soft drinks,
who eat white bread, who eat refined sugar and
so on." Though her bone cancer may actually
have had nothing to do with her eating habits,
she blamed it on the "junk food" she had eaten
before shifting in the 1950s to a diet emphasizing
whole-grain bread, fresh fruit and vegetables,
fish, liver, milk, and eggs.

Davis died of her cancer in 1974, at the age
of seventy, after expressing the hope that her
disease would not discourage people from following the nutritional advice in her books. Sadly, her
own self-criticism in the months before her death
may have done just that. Though no evidence has
linked Davis's cancer with her diet, her own reaction to her illness helped give rise to later rumors as the news of her death spread.

Similar rumors of death from stomach cancer
have attached themselves to Euell Gibbons, the
popular wild food expert. His first and perhaps
most famous book, *Stalking the Wild Asparagus,*
introduced many to the wild delicacies to be found
growing in our fields and forests. In the summer
of 1974, newspapers reported that Gibbons had

developed an ulcer. He quickly assured his readers that it was probably due to the aspirin he took for an arthritic condition and not to the milkweed shoots and dandelion greens that he recommended in his books. But when he died of natural causes a year later, rumors blamed the death on his diet.

Jim Fixx, another well-known health advocate, really did die from his recommended exercise—long-distance running. The author of *The Complete Book of Running*, Fixx died of a heart attack while running along a Vermont road in 1984. He was fifty-two. Though the run on the day of his death seems to have brought on his heart attack, it is likely that his exercise program actually prolonged his life.

Fixx took up running at the age of thirty-five, in part because of fears that he might follow the path of his father, who had died of a heart attack at forty-three. He was overweight when he began running, his father's death made him a likely candidate for heart problems, and he had smoked for a number of years. Taken together, Fixx's health outlook at thirty-five was not promising. His running helped him to lose weight and stop smoking, and it probably helped to strengthen his circulatory system. But Fixx seems to have relied too heavily on the running to improve his heart, neglecting changes he might have made in his diet. In a 1979 interview in the *London Daily Mail*, he boasted that he had breakfasted on fried eggs, sausage, bacon, buttered toast, and coffee with cream. He managed to stay thin while eating such food, but the fats eventually clogged his heart. After his death, doctors discovered that both his right and left coronary arteries were severely blocked and that a third was nearly fifty percent closed. Fixx's death showed that exercise alone can't keep a person healthy, and that without care and attention to the body's warning signals, the added stress of exercise can actually trigger a heart attack.

★ ★ Claus von Bülow killed his mother and kept her on ice in his home. (1984)

Not true. This is one of several entirely false rumors that circulated about Claus von Bülow while he was being tried for the attempted murder of his wife, Sunny, and during his retrial. Von Bülow emerged from those proceedings a free man with a shadowy past. According to Dominick Dunne, the author of an August 1985 *Vanity Fair* article about the acquitted man, perverse rumors have circulated about von Bülow for most of his life. These have included stories that he is a necrophile, that he was a page boy at Hermann Göring's wedding, and that he was at one time involved in international espionage. Von Bülow denies the rumors, and says that the necrophilia story began as a joke told on Capri in 1949 by Prince Dado Ruspoli and Fiat owner Gianni Agnelli.

★ ★ Queen Victoria collected photographs of the dead bodies of her friends and relatives. When she died, her private rooms were found filled with hundreds of the pictures. (1901)

Partly true. Queen Victoria did have a fascination with death, though this was not uncommon in the nineteenth century. When her husband, Albert, the prince consort, died in 1861, she went into mourning, which was to last until her own death in 1901. For forty years she wore black, and each year on the anniversary of Albert's death she held a private service at his grave and spent the day alone. She had his bedroom at Windsor photographed from every angle so that it could be cleaned and maintained exactly as it had been while he was alive. Though no visitors were allowed to stay in the room, sheets and towels were changed regularly, the prince consort's clothes were laid out daily, and hot water was brought up each evening. For forty years the Queen wore a bracelet that held a portrait of Albert and a lock of his hair. She also kept a photograph of Albert, taken after death, beside her bed.

Victoria's biographers mention no other postmortem photographs, and it seems as though Albert's picture has flourished in the popular imagination. We must note in Victoria's defense that though such an intense interest in death may seem odd today, it was quite common a century ago. The death chambers of the well-to-do were often kept untouched for years, and many people in all walks of life had photographs made of dead loved ones. The Victorians were deeply religious and had a highly romantic interest in the moment of passing into the afterworld. The literature of the last century was as preoccupied with death as ours is with sex.

★ ★ B. F. Skinner, the behavioral psychologist, raised his daughter in a "Skinner Box." She was so traumatized by the experience that she grew up to be psychotic and suicidal. When she turned twenty-one she sued her father for damages. (1960s)

Not true. B. F. Skinner built a climate-controlled crib for his second daughter, Deborah, when she was born in 1944. The unit was essentially a large version of the baby incubators commonly used in hospitals and was designed to allow Deborah to live comfortably through a Minnesota winter without being wrapped in layers of clothing and blankets. Far from being unhappy in her crib, which her father called the "baby tender," Deborah seems to have been an unusually contented baby. When his daughter was seven months old, Skinner reported to a colleague, "She has never shown any sign of not wanting to be put back and simply does not cry. For the first three months she would cry when wet, but would stop immediately upon changing....The only times she has cried in the past four months (and this is literally true) have been when she had diphtheria shots (and then only for a minute or two), when I nipped the tip of her finger while trimming her nails, and once or twice when we have taken her bottle away to adjust the nipple!" Because she lived unconstricted by outer clothing, Deborah was also relatively free from rashes.

Deborah Skinner in the baby tender, age eleven months   Photograph by Stuart

In October 1945, when Deborah was just over a year old, the *Ladies' Home Journal* printed an article about the crib under the headline "Baby in a Box." A picture showed Deborah in a smaller, portable version of the crib, with her hands pressed against the glass. Hundreds of new and expecting parents wrote for instructions for building their own baby tenders. (Skinner eventually made arrangements to sell the cribs commercially, under the trade names "Heir Conditioner" and "Aircrib," but without much success.) Other parents wrote in outrage that babies should not be caged and experimented on like animals.

Most of the angry letters came from people who had not seen the article, but had only heard about it. In retelling, Skinner's crib apparently became confused with his earlier behavior-testing apparatus, the "Skinner Box," used for studying learning behavior in rats and pigeons. In fact, Skinner did not perform behavior experiments on his daughter. The baby tender was used simply to keep her warm and comfortable, and both parents regularly took her out for play and feeding.

Deborah continued to sleep in the crib until she was two and a half, then led a fairly normal life out of the public eye. Now forty-two, she lives in London with her husband and works as an artist. She has never been psychotic or suicidal, and she remains close to her father. Her years in the baby tender seem to have done her no harm, though the rumors, which started years later, have sometimes bothered her. In a 1971 interview she recalled, "My father was very concerned about these rumors, as was I. He thinks they may have affected me. After college, I had a typical half-year of depression, the sort of identity crisis that everybody I've ever known has gone through. At this point my father brought up the idea that I don't have enough faith in myself, and that the rumors may have something to do with this." She is now able to laugh the stories aside, and in a more recent interview joked, "I'm pretty sure I'm not crazy. And I don't seem to have committed suicide."

Courtesy B. F. Skinner

Deborah Skinner in London, age forty-two

★ ★ Joan Crawford made a pornographic movie early in her acting career. After she became a star, Louis B. Mayer bought up the surviving copies to protect her screen image. (1930s)

Unconfirmed. Rumors of such a film plagued Joan Crawford throughout her life, and to date no evidence has been found to prove or disprove the story. Informed sources tend to discount it as mere rumor, pointing out that the reel has never surfaced. But to those who believe the story, the absence of the film only confirms that all copies were destroyed. The most common version of the rumor gives the film's title as *The Casting Couch*, with a "plot" that involves a young actress applying for a movie role. Her screen test includes a number of sexual acts. Since nobody on record has seen the film, however, such details can only be part of the myth. Perhaps the wildest version of the story claims that the single surviving copy is owned by an Austrian count who spends his lecherous evenings screening the film again and again.

Bob Thomas, in his 1978 biography, *Joan Crawford*, reports that the actress received a telephone call one night in 1935 from a man who claimed to have a copy of the film, which he was willing to sell at a steep price. She referred the caller to Louis B. Mayer and MGM's attorney, J. Robert Rubin. According to Thomas, both men saw the film and agreed that the woman in it was *not* Joan Crawford. It isn't clear from his text where Thomas got this story, and it may well be another elaboration of the rumor.

Arthur Knight, an expert on sex in the movies and a longtime contributor to *Playboy* magazine, is of the opinion that Joan Crawford never made a stag film. His conclusion is based on the complete absence of copies: "*Playboy* pays a lot of money to acquire pornographic films; you'd think that if a Joan Crawford stag reel existed, one would have been offered for sale." Knight has also searched through the huge collection of blue movies at the Kinsey Institute in Bloomington, Indiana, without finding the alleged Crawford footage.

★ ★ Clint Eastwood is the son of comedian Stan Laurel.

Not true, though coincidence and secrecy make this story less farfetched than it might seem. Clint Eastwood keeps a tight lid on information about his private life, and this close-mouthed attitude toward the press and the public has created an element of mystery around the actor that has undoubtedly fueled the rumor. Eastwood's biographical listing in *Who's Who in America* makes no mention of his parents (a highly unusual omission) and gives his birthdate as May 31, without specifying the year. Elsewhere, however, he has revealed that he was born in San Francisco in 1930, and that his father's name was also Clinton.

In 1930 Stan Laurel was at the pinnacle of his film career and his marriage was failing. On May 7—the same month that Clint Eastwood was born—his wife gave birth to a son in Hollywood. The child was born two months prematurely and lived only nine days. Laurel, who could not bear to attend funerals, insisted on a cremation.

Somehow, the infant's death without a funeral in 1930 and Clint Eastwood's reluctance as an adult to expose his family to the spotlight of publicity have combined to make one of our more curious rumors.

Clint Eastwood

Stan Laurel

★ ★ When Lauren Bacall sings in the film *To Have and Have Not*, the voice we hear is actually the dubbed-in crooning of the fourteen-year-old Andy Williams. (1950s)

Unconfirmed. We've read this little nugget in trivia books and in a biography of Bacall and watched it rattled off as fact on the television show "Ripley's Believe It or Not." It makes a good story and almost always draws a chuckle; unfortunately, it is probably not true.

To Have and Have Not, released in 1944, was Lauren Bacall's first Hollywood film and her first big break as an actress. In it she sings two songs, "Am I Blue?" and "How Little We Know." Because of the way the songs were shot, both had to be recorded in a sound studio and then mouthed to a playback in front of the cameras, so both are essentially dubbed. The question is, who did the singing? Bacall has always maintained that she sang the songs herself. In her autobiography, *By Myself*, she describes the filming of the song "How Little We Know," and director Howard Hawks's reaction to her work.

> I had pre-recorded the song and was to sing the playback, which is not easy, particularly for a novice. Howard was satisfied with the recording, though he thought one or two notes might have to be dubbed later on. . . . At the end of that long day, Howard put his arm around me and said, "You did a really good day's work, Betty, I'm proud of you." That's the only true compliment he ever paid me.

Bacall's lip-synch acting for the song deserved the praise. The match of the voice to the movement of her lips is practically flawless, even during a brief close-up shot of her face. Her acting during the song "Am I Blue?" did not have to be so precise. She only sang a few lines, and in half of them she was filmed from behind so that her face did not show.

The story that the singing voice in the film actually belonged to an adolescent boy probably sprang from Bacall's unusually low-pitched speaking voice. Another rumor claimed that her distinctive growl came from months spent yelling at the top of her lungs in remote mountain parks. *Time* magazine repeated this tale with the added flourish that she'd once been caught in the act by two policemen and that only a hasty explanation had kept them from dragging her into the local station.

We believe Bacall's claim to her own singing voice in *To Have and Have Not*, but we haven't been able to prove that Andy Williams did not contribute some notes. He has never spoken up on the matter, and he did not answer our phone calls and letters. Williams would have been fourteen years old in 1944, a perfect match to the rumor, and, from 1938 to 1947, he sang with three brothers as the Williams Brothers Quartet for radio stations in Des Moines, Chicago, Cincinnati, and Los Angeles. That means that he was a professional singer at the time and that he may well have been in Los Angeles during the filming of *To Have and Have Not*.

In Lauren Bacall's defense, we should note that she has proved herself to be a talented singer in the years since the rumor first appeared. In

1970 she starred in the Broadway musical, *Applause,* and her singing voice was good enough to earn her a Tony award for her performance.

━━━━━━━━━━━━━━━━━━━━━━━━━━━━━

★★ Richard Simmons, the exercise celebrity, is really in his early sixties. He looks much younger because he's had plastic surgery and hair transplants. (1984)

Not true. Richard Simmons was thirty-six years old in 1984, when this rumor ran rampant. But he is a changeling of sorts. The former actor was once so fat that a list of his acting roles sounds more like a menu than a résumé: he played a dancing meatball in one television commercial, a Dannon yogurt in another, and was cast by director Federico Fellini in a food-orgy scene in the film *Satyricon.* Moved to diet by an anonymous note left on the windshield of his car that said "Dear Richard, Fat people die young. Please don't die," Simmons lost 112 pounds in less than three months. He then underwent plastic surgery to have three inches of loose skin removed from his face. The enterprising Simmons soon turned his triumph over flab into a successful career: his syndicated television show plays coast to coast, his self-help books have reached best-sellerdom, and his nationally franchised "Anatomy Asylum" exercise salons are thunderously successful.

★ ★ Alfonso Ribeiro, the child who danced as a miniature Michael Jackson in the Pepsi commercial, died from a break-dancing injury. (1984)

Not true. Alfonso Ribeiro is still very much alive and dancing. He filmed the Pepsi-Cola commercial in the spring of 1984, at the age of twelve, during time off from his starring role in the Broadway show *The Tap Dance Kid.* Just a year earlier, Ribeiro had been an ordinary seventh grader at Junior High School 141 in the Bronx. But his friends and family knew that he could dance, and his teachers sent him to audition for *The Tap Dance Kid* when they heard the show needed a young hoofer. He got the part, earned rave reviews when the show opened, and got a chance to work with Michael Jackson on the Pepsi commercial.

The rumors that spring of Ribeiro's break-dancing death were slowed by his publicity appearances on television shows like "Donahue" and by a piece in *People* magazine in July, but some storytellers have clung to the tale.

For some peculiar reason, child actors have become a regular target of untimely death stories. Jerry Mathers, who played the Beaver on the series "Leave It to Beaver," was rumored to have died in Vietnam in 1968 (*Rumor!*, page 74). He didn't, but he still finds himself denying the old story. The little boy who played Mikey on the Life cereal commercial was rumored to have died from eating carbonated candy in 1978 (*Rumor!*, page 68). He didn't die either. Nor was the boy in the St. Joseph's aspirin commercial ("Mommies are like that. Yeah, they are.") killed when his mother supposedly backed over him with the family car. And Buffy, the daughter on "Family Affair," did not die from getting her scarf caught in the wheel of a school bus.

The rumor of Alfonso Ribeiro's death is probably tied to the publicity given to the danger of break dancing in the spring of 1984. Ribeiro did do some fancy "breaking" in both the Pepsi commercial and *The Tap Dance Kid*. A January 1984 *Newsweek* review of the Broadway show noted that he "dances like an urban whirlwind, not only tapping but disassembling his bone structure in that joyous human puppetry of the streets known as 'breaking.'" (Perhaps some readers took that colorful wording literally.) By the late spring, the fad for break dancing had resulted in so many accidents that the media began to warn the untrained and out-of-shape from attempting the more difficult moves. In an interview in *People*, Dr. Jack Bertman of the Los Angeles Orthopaedic Hospital said that he was seeing "an average of one break dance injury each day, sometimes more." The most common injuries were "to the back and lower neck—strains and sprains." The magazine *Scientific American* summarized accidents reported by doctors around the country in a March 1985 article. Several severe spinal injuries were on the list, as well as many broken arms, legs, fingers, and toes, and a few cases of patchy baldness caused by head spinning.

The Alfonso Ribeiro rumor may also have started as a simple confusion of names. In the fall of 1983, a rookie lineman for the Pittsburgh

Steelers named Gabriel Rivera was paralyzed from the chest down as the result of an automobile accident. The similarity between the two names could well be the cause of the rumor.

★ ★ When Paul McCartney was busted in Japan in 1980, police discovered that his fingerprints did not match those on file from the 1960s. This is why he was held for ten days and proves once and for all that the real Paul died in 1966. (1980)

Not true. The story only proves that some old rumors never die. Most of us thought we'd heard the last of Paul McCartney's secret death and replacement when the rumor faded away in the spring of 1970 (see *Rumor!*, page 82). But some ardent believers still cling to the story, and reports of another "clue" in 1980 were enough to revive the whole affair, though this time around the story got far less attention.

On January 16, 1980, Paul McCartney was arrested at Tokyo International Airport for possession of just under half a pound of marijuana. He was taken to a jail cell at the Tokyo Metropolitan Police Department while the district prosecutor decided what should be done. McCartney followed the daily regimen of an ordinary Japanese prisoner; he slept on a floor mat, rose with the other prisoners at 6:00 A.M., sat cross-legged for roll call (shouting "hai" when his number was called), and used the communal bath. He was detained for ten days while prosecutors checked on his background, then he was deported to England.

According to the rumor, the ten-day holding period was unusually long and was caused by the confusion over McCartney's fingerprints. In fact, by Japanese law he could have been held for up to twenty days before being arraigned, and, if convicted, he might have faced a sentence of up to seven years. McCartney was lucky to have been released as quickly as he was and to have left the country with no criminal charges against him.

★ ★ Glenn Miller did not die in a plane crash over the English Channel as reported, but was shot by a jealous lover in Paris. (1945)

Not true. Glenn Miller was at the height of his popularity when he disappeared in 1944, and his mournful fans have honored his memory with scores of curious stories of his fate. The true story was apparently not dramatic enough to satisfy people's needs.

While all the facts of Miller's death may never be ascertained, it is known that he left England for Paris in a single-engine C-64 military plane on December 15, 1944. Neither he nor anyone else aboard the plane was ever seen again. Since the weather was wet, foggy, and hovering at about the freezing point, it has long been assumed that the plane suffered from icing problems and went down in the English Channel. The C-64 had no de-icing equipment.

The many rumors undoubtedly sprang from the lack of hard evidence of the crash and from the time it took to discover that anything was wrong. The rest of Miller's band was held up in England by the weather and did not arrive in Paris until December 18. Only then did they realize that Miller was missing. It took several more days before anyone found out that the plane had been lost. Miller's wife was finally notified on December 23 that her husband was "missing in flight." For many months she clung to the hope that he would eventually turn up alive.

Rumors began to circulate almost as soon as news of Miller's disappearance became public. Some said he'd been killed in a brawl in a Paris brothel or he'd been shot by a jealous lover. Others claimed he was still alive, disfigured from the accident and embarrassed to show himself in public. According to one story, the other officer on the flight was about to be arrested for black-market dealings. To avoid capture he had killed Miller and the pilot and escaped in the plane by himself.

In 1986, some fresh information about Miller's fate was revealed by two crew members of a British plane that flew over the Channel on a bombing mission the day of the disappearance.

The mission had been called off and the planes ordered to jettison their bombs. According to Fred Shaw, the navigator, after one of the bombs exploded the crew saw a C-64 go down into the sea, apparently jarred by the force of the blast. Victor Gregory, the pilot of the plane that dropped the bomb, confirmed the story when a Miller fan tracked him down through an ad in the RAF Association magazine. "It was an accident and we were sorry," Gregory recalled, "but nothing could be done about it. And there was no debriefing at which to report it because the mission was aborted." Two forty-year-old memories are thin threads on which to hang conclusions about Miller's fate, but it is possible that his plane was accidentally downed by a British bomb.

━━━━━━━━━━━━━━━━━━━━━━━━━━━━━━━

★ ★ L. Ron Hubbard, founder of the Church of Scientology, died in 1980. (1982)

Not true. L. Ron Hubbard died in 1986, but the last few years of his life are shrouded in mystery. He disappeared in March 1980, at the same time that a new group took control of the highest positions in the church and began to demand bigger fees from the church's regional franchise owners. For the next six years, Hubbard kept his whereabouts a closely guarded secret. He was not seen again by his family members or by former close associates within the church. In 1982, his son, Ronald E. DeWolf, brought a lawsuit against the church, claiming that his father was dead or mentally incompetent and that Hubbard's personal assets were being siphoned off by the new church leaders.

Hubbard never appeared at the trial that was to rule on his existence. Instead he sent a single signed and fingerprinted statement to the effect that he remained in hiding of his own free will because he had received death threats. The judge decided that the letter was sufficient evidence and in May 1983 ruled that L. Ron Hubbard was still alive.

Hubbard's death in 1986 was handled with the same mysteriousness that cloaked his last years of life. On Saturday, January 25, county officials in San Louis Obispo, California, were notified that Hubbard had died the day before at a remote retreat in Creston. Church officials presented the county coroner with a statement signed by Hubbard stating that for religious reasons he did not want an autopsy performed. County officials were allowed only to photograph and fingerprint the body. Dr. Eugene Denk, Hubbard's personal physician for many years and himself a Scientologist, drew up the death certificate, which listed the cause of death as a stroke. Hubbard's body was then cremated and the ashes scattered at sea.

★ ★ Calvin Coolidge's son died from wearing black socks. The poison dye entered his bloodstream through a cut on his foot. (1924)

Not true. President Coolidge's son died in 1924, at the age of sixteen, from blood poisoning caused by an infected blister on his foot. The death had nothing to do with black socks. The younger Calvin Coolidge had played tennis wearing sneakers without socks and had developed a blister on top of one of his toes. Soon the toe had become infected and swollen. With modern antibiotics, such a wound would be of little concern, but in 1924 a bad infection was a serious medical matter. Doctors did what they could, but, by the time they were called, the infection was out of control. The boy died on July 7, about two weeks after he had developed the blister.

The rumor about black socks somehow attached itself to the story of young Coolidge's death and has survived as a sort of teenage legend. The death was of special interest to teenagers because of the boy's age, and it has largely been teenagers who have spread the rumor about black socks in the years since. This may simply be the result of youthful anxiety about dress and appearance.

The worry about poisoning from dyed socks may have had its source in the real toxins that were sometimes used to color clothing in the early part of the century. Zinc chloride was often used to give a pearl-gray color to socks and other clothes, and the unabsorbed dye in new garments sometimes caused skin inflammation. Even more toxic was anilin black, frequently used to color shoe leather. Medical journals from the turn of the century contain reports of children who lost consciousness after absorbing anilin dye through their skin from freshly polished shoes.

★ ★ The Lindbergh baby is still alive. The body discovered was that of another child. (1932)

Not true. On May 12, 1932, two months after the Lindbergh baby was kidnapped, a child's body was found in a shallow grave several miles from the Lindbergh home. The child had been dead for about two months, but its features were well enough preserved that Charles Lindbergh identified it at once as his son. The child's nursemaid also saw the body and agreed that it was her charge. Its blond curly hair matched samples saved by the parents as keepsakes, and two of its toes had the distinctive overlap of the missing child. When found, the body was clothed in a blue flannel nightshirt made by the Lindbergh's nursemaid from a petticoat. The fabric and scalloped edge of the nightshirt matched scraps saved from the petticoat.

During the trial of Bruno Richard Hauptmann, the accused kidnapper, the defense counsel tried halfheartedly to question the identity of the body. Then, partway through the trial, the chief defense attorney bowed to the state's positive identification. His associate in the case angrily blurted, "You are conceding Hauptmann to the electric chair!" and stormed from the courtroom. After Hauptmann was sentenced to death for the kidnapping, many backseat lawyers thought that more could have been done to raise the corpse's identity as an issue. They pointed to the four-inch discrepancy between the corpse's length as reported by the coroner and the baby's height as reported by the state police. And to counter the evidence of the overlapping toes, they pointed to the examining coroner's testimony at a related trial that both feet were missing from the corpse. Perhaps the defense could have done more to raise doubt about the body's identification in the minds of the jury, but the evidence of the nightshirt, coupled with the declarations of the father and nursemaid, seem to have already settled the issue.

When the baby was first kidnapped, another rumor suggested that the parents themselves might have been behind the abduction—that the child was an idiot or somehow defective and that the Lindberghs wanted to be rid of it. Photographs of the baby show that it was perfectly normal, and a doctor who examined the child two weeks before the crime found no defects.

★ ★ The nursery rhyme "Ring Around the Rosy" dates back to the 1606 outbreak of plague in London. "Rosy" refers to the flushed look of those afflicted with the plague. The line "pocket full of posies" describes the sweet-smelling flowers and herbs people carried to ward off the disease. "Ashes, ashes" is a distortion of the sound of sneezing, a common symptom of the plague, and "we all fall down" is a clear reference to death.

Not true. "Ring Around the Rosy" first appeared in print in 1881 as a rhyme in Kate Greenaway's *Mother Goose*. None of the many earlier collections of nursery rhymes mentions the verse, and there is absolutely no evidence connecting it to the plague. *The Oxford Dictionary of Nursery Rhymes* somewhat haughtily notes that "the invariable sneezing and falling down in modern versions has given would-be origin-finders the opportunity to say that the rhyme dates back to the days of the Great Plague." Greenaway's original version reads:

Ring-a-ring-a-roses,
A pocket full of posies;
Hush! Hush! Hush! Hush!
We've all tumbled down.

The story connecting this rhyme with the plague is undoubtedly influenced by scholarly efforts to link other rhymes with historical events and figures. "High Diddle, Diddle," for example, has been the subject of a great deal of speculation. Various scholars have suggested that the line "the cat ran away with the spoon" describes

Queen Elizabeth I of England (who may have been nicknamed "The Cat" for her skill at manipulating her cabinet), Catherine of Aragon (called Catherine la Fidele), or Catherine the Great of Russia. *The Oxford Dictionary of Nursery Rhymes* dismisses all these theories as nonsense. "Humpty Dumpty" and "The Old Woman Who Lived in a Shoe" are supposed by some to refer to the spread and fragmentation of the British Empire, but again the theories rely only on evidence found in the wording of the poems.

With very few exceptions, the attempts to find historical foundations in nursery rhymes rely on assumption and speculation. In fairness to the theorists, we should note that a few of the poems probably do refer to historical figures. "Old King Cole" is almost certainly about a popular British king who ruled in the third century, and "Good Queen Bess was a glorious dame / When bonny King Jemmy from Scotland came" refers to Queen Elizabeth I and her choice of James V as her successor.

★ ★ If you put a troll doll in the freezer its hair will grow. (1963)

Not true. A fad for troll dolls, also known as "Dam Things" and "Dammit Dolls," swept the country in the early 1960s, accompanied by the story that if you put your troll doll in the freezer overnight its hair would grow. This sounds like a tale invented to console a child who wanted a "Tressy"—the teen doll who had hair that grew when you turned the knob between her shoulder blades—but got a little troll instead.

When we put our troll doll in the freezer overnight its hair froze to the ice cube tray and tore out when we tried to pry it off.

★ ★ A woman who bought a Cabbage Patch Kid doll discovered that its arm was not attached properly; in fact, it fell off after a few days. She sent the doll back to the manufacturer to be repaired, and two weeks later received a death certificate in the mail. (1983)

Not true. Coleco Industries, manufacturer of Cabbage Patch dolls, assures us that this is just a story—and one that they consider to be in poor taste. According to the company, if a purchaser did have a serious problem with one of the dolls, Coleco's customer-service department would either repair the defect or replace the doll.

Cabbage Patch dolls come with adoption papers, a feature that has given the dolls a tremendous appeal by making them seem like real babies. The rumor extends that realism with a sinister twist.

While Cabbage Patch dolls don't get death certificates, they can go to a special Cabbage Patch summer camp in New Jersey, and a dentist in Arlington, Texas, will fit them with orthodontic braces.

★ ★ Members of the rock group Kiss worship the devil. The group's name stands for "Knights in Satan's Service." (1980)

Not true. Kiss has never been a group for sweet Christian harmony, but neither has it been involved in devil worship. The many rumors about the group are a classic demonstration of the theory that rumors flourish in the absence of real information. When a curious public is denied the facts, it often invents its own.

Kiss was formed in 1973 by four New York City musicians—Gene Simmons, Paul Stanley, Ace Frehley, and Peter Criss. From the beginning, the group's trademark was facial makeup. The musicians always appeared on stage in bizarre white and black greasepaint, which not only made them look strange, but kept their true identities from their fans. When drummer Peter Criss left the group in 1980 (he was replaced by Eric Carr) he was able to walk away with his private life intact. Though the band's records had sold millions of copies, not even the most devoted fan could recognize him on the street. As Simmons put it, "If you want to be Superman, you can't let everybody know you're Clark Kent."

The privacy and mystery gave rise to speculation and then to rumor. Fans wanted to know more about the group, and when the information wasn't forthcoming, stories began to surface. The group's black humor and unusual theatrics—Simmons sometimes played a guitar that looked like a bloody executioner's ax—led to rumors of satanism. Gene Simmons's long tongue, which he can extend an inch below his chin, was rumored to have been surgically altered. Some thought the connecting skin beneath his tongue had been clipped, others whispered he'd had a cow's tongue inserted in place of his own. One story claimed Frehley was the secretly returned Jim Morrison, the lead singer of the Doors who died in 1971. A Kiss comic book was rumored to have been printed with blood.

Members of the band have repeatedly denied all these rumors. They have since revealed their ungreased faces, and they no longer try to conceal their true identities. But once started, rumors are hard to stop, and it is likely that the Kiss stories will be around as long as the group is active.

Members of the group Kiss, Gene Simmons displaying his tongue

★ ★ The rock group AC/DC is involved in devil worship. The name stands for "Anti-Christ/Devil's Children." (1985)

Not true. The rumor appeared not long after Richard Ramirez was arrested in 1985 and charged with the multiple murders known as the Night Stalker killings in El Paso, Texas. A neighbor told the press that Ramirez had been obsessed with the song "Night Prowler" from AC/DC's 1979 *Highway to Hell* album. Those anxious about the unwholesome messages of modern rock songs seized on this as further reason for worry, and before long the inevitable charge of satanism had been leveled against the group.

Brothers Malcolm and Angus Young started AC/DC in 1973, and, like Kiss, the band is loud, raucous, and anything but sweet. But it has nothing to do with devil worship. The name came from the markings on the back of a radio that belonged to the Youngs' little sister. It stands for "alternating current/direct current." The group picked the name because it suggests power, and they have come to be known for their supercharged, high-decibel performances.

In the past few years, charges of satanism have been leveled against a number of rock groups. While the accusations are largely unfounded, suggestions of satanism in band names, song titles, and lyrics are not uncommon. AC/DC's choice of *Highway to Hell* as an album title may well have been at the root of the later rumor of satanism. Other examples of satanic references include the name of the group Black Sabbath, the

Rolling Stones's song "Sympathy for the Devil" and their album *Their Satanic Majesties Request*, and Santana's song "Black Magic Woman."

★★ The circular peace symbol is a satanic device, designed by Communists as part of a plot to subvert the free world. (1970)

Not true. The peace symbol was created by a young British designer named Gerald Holtam in 1958 for a group called the Campaign for Nuclear Disarmament. The CND was formed that year to oppose Britain's plan to develop and test its own nuclear bomb. The symbol's design is based on the semaphore signals for the letters N and D, standing for "Nuclear Disarmament." It was adopted in the 1960s by a broad range of antiwar and nuclear disarmament groups and eventually came to be associated in the United States with protest against the Vietnam War.

One of the first rumors about the peace symbol circulated in California in 1967 and alleged that the design stood for "free love." By the mid-1960s, the mark was so widely used that it became a sort of vague emblem of the counterculture, so the story is not too farfetched. But in

1970 a much stranger story began to make the rounds: the symbol was actually a satanic device, maliciously designed by Communists. The source of this story seems to be an article by David Gumaer published in the June 1970 issue of the John Birch Society's *American Opinion*. Titled "Peace Symbols: The Truth about Those Strange Designs," Gumaer's article links the Campaign for Nuclear Disarmament, communism, and satanism in an adroitly written essay that relies heavily on misinformation to drive its points home. For instance, Gumaer states that Bertrand Russell designed the symbol and puts great emphasis on Russell's Communist sympathies as evidence against the emblem. Russell was in fact one of the founding members of the Campaign for Nuclear Disarmament, and his leftist leanings had involved him with Communists from time to time in his life, but he did not design the peace symbol.

Much of Gumaer's attention in his article is devoted to the portion of the symbol inside the circle. Since the peace symbol in its entirety was a new device, Gumaer had to pull it apart to find a sinister past. He refers to the center portion as a "chicken track" or "swept-wing bomber in vertical flight," and goes on to connect it with the cross on which St. Peter was crucified upside down. According to Gumaer, the "chicken track" became a symbol of anti-Christian sentiment and was used in satanic rituals to represent the opposite of the cross. Even if this is true, it has little to do with the creation of the peace symbol, which was designed by a young artist as a simple device for a group seeking an end to nuclear weaponry.

We might also point out that it can be misleading to put too much weight on the ancient meanings of symbols; modern use can eclipse centuries of tradition. The Nabisco trademark was derived from a medieval device that once meant the triumph of good over evil, but few people today would connect it with anything other than cookies and crackers. And the swastika was at one time a widely recognized symbol of well-being and prosperity. Its adoption by the Nazis changed that meaning profoundly.

★ ★ A devil baby, with cloven hooves, pointed ears, and a tail, was born at Jane Addams's Hull House in Chicago. (1916)

Not true. The residents of Hull House first learned of this rumor when three women appeared at the door demanding to see the child. The women knew just what the baby looked like and had heard how it swore profusely from the moment it was born. In spite of the settlement house's most sincere denials, the women went away convinced that the baby was being hidden in a room inside.

Over the next several weeks Hull House received hundreds of visitors who wanted to see the child, and the workers there heard many variations on the tale. In one version, the baby was born into a family with six daughters. When the mother became pregnant for the seventh time, her husband angrily said that he'd rather have a devil than another daughter. And that's just what he got. In another version, the mother—a deeply religious woman—put a holy picture on the bedroom wall. Her husband—an atheist—tore it down, saying that he'd prefer a devil in the house to such nonsense. Nine months later his wish was granted. Addams related the legend in an article for *Atlantic Monthly*, describing how, according to the story, the infant ended up at Hull House:

> As soon as the Devil Baby was born, he ran about the table shaking his finger in deep reproach at his father, who finally caught him and in fear and trembling brought him to Hull-House. When the residents there, in spite of the baby's shocking appearance, wishing to save his soul, took him to church for baptism, they found that the shawl was empty and the Devil Baby, fleeing from the holy water, ran lightly over the backs of the pews.

In another version of the story, the newborn infant grabbed the cigar from his father's mouth and took a few puffs before letting loose with foul language.

Jane Addams was intrigued by the tale, and spent as much time as she could talking with visitors to explain that it wasn't true. She was amazed that such a medieval-sounding story could thrive in a modern city, but on reflection she realized that the legend of the devil baby had served as a moral tale—the story of a wayward husband brought to justice. Most of the visitors were women, eager to see the punishment meted out to the evil man, and many had brought their own husbands along so that the message would be driven home.

The legend of Hull House's devil baby lost momentum after a few months, but an almost identical tale has been kept alive in New Jersey for more than a century, largely as a local amusement. According to what has become the "official" version of the legend, the Jersey Devil was born in 1735 to a Mrs. Leeds of Estellville. Like the Hull House devil baby, the Jersey Devil came as punishment for a loose tongue, but in this story it was the mother who spoke recklessly. Pregnant for the thirteenth time, Mrs. Leeds angrily told a friend that she'd as soon have a devil as another baby. She got her wish in a dramatic way. Her child was born with cloven hooves, an animal's head, and wings. It stood up after the birth, swore at its mother, and flew up the chimney and out into the wilds of the New Jersey pine barrens.

Through the years, the legend of the Jersey Devil has been kept alive by carnival hucksters and newspaper hoaxers, as well as by respectable citizens who report sighting it from time to time. The storied creature has been around since the late nineteenth century—it was spotted in Bridgeton in 1873, and tracks were found near Leeds Point in 1894—but it was in the first decade of this century that it earned widespread notoriety. In 1906, showman Norman Jeffries concocted a scheme to bring crowds to his Arch Street Museum in Philadelphia. He planted a story of a Jersey Devil sighting in a small rural paper, then arranged the capture of a live specimen. The report of the sighting piqued the public's interest, and the capture caused a sensation. Huge crowds arrived at Jeffries's museum to see the creature, and most went away satisfied and amazed. It later turned out that the Arch Street devil was just a kangaroo painted with green stripes and fitted with a pair of bronze wings, but the hoax served to pump new life into an old legend.

In 1909 the Jersey Devil was spotted by dozens of terrified citizens across western New Jersey and eastern Pennsylvania. Postmaster E. W. Minster of Bristol, Pennsylvania, saw the creature in the early morning hours of January 17 and described it in detail:

> As I got up I heard an eerie, almost supernatural sound from the direction of the river. . . I looked out upon the Delaware and saw flying diagonally across what appeared to be a large crane but which was emitting a glow like a firefly. Its head resembled that of a ram, with curled horns, and its long thin neck was thrust forward in flight. It had long thin wings and short legs, the front legs shorter than the hind. Again, it uttered its mournful and awful call—a combination of a squawk and a whistle, the beginning very high and piercing and ending very low and hoarse.

That same evening, a police officer in Bristol fired two shots at a strange creature as it flew overhead, and a liquor dealer looked out his window to see the monster standing in the tow path on the bank of the Delaware Division Canal. Residents of Trenton, New Jersey, were also kept on edge that month by strange screeching noises over the Delaware River and by peculiar hoof prints found in the snow.

Since 1909, there have been occasional, widely scattered Jersey Devil sightings and some Halloween hoaxes, but the legend has been kept alive as an entertaining bit of local lore. While the monster has largely been turned into a sanitized creature fit for modern tourist brochures, its original legend seems to spring from a genuinely ancient folklore tradition. The tale of the casual remark that spawned a devil is essentially the same one that arose around Chicago's Hull House in 1915. And Lady Gregory, gathering folk stories in the west of Ireland in the years before World War I, was told much the same story by one of her sources there:

> Some say the evil eye is in those who were baptised wrong, but I believe it's not that, but when a woman is carrying, some one that meets her says, "So you're in that way," and she says, "The devil a fear of me," as even a married woman might say for sport or not to let on, the devil gets possession of the child at that moment, and when it is born it has the evil eye.

A similar tale with just as long a pedigree describes how an expectant mother, frightened by a black cat, gave birth to a devil baby complete with horns, tail, and teeth. The idea that a fetus in the womb can be transformed by a mother's thoughts has given rise to a host of related stories. A mother who watched a criminal tortured on the rack is said to have given birth to an infant with broken bones. More recently a battered baby is said to have been delivered to a woman who witnessed a terrible car accident, or who saw a crippled person or circus freak during her pregnancy.

When Jane Addams encountered the story of the devil baby at Hull House, she was very likely hearing a story that had been told for hundreds of years. She was amazed that such a bizarre tale could find so many believers in a twentieth-century American city. It seems just as surprising today—until we consider the popularity of the film *Rosemary's Baby* and remember that in 1985 Procter & Gamble decided to drop its moon-and-stars trademark from consumer packages because of a wild (and completely unfounded) rumor that the firm was involved in devil worship (see *Rumor!*, page 144). We haven't really left the Salem witch trials far behind us.

★ ★ The theme song to the television show "Mr. Ed," when played backward, contains the messages "the source is Satan" and "someone sung this song for Satan." (1986)

Not true. Evangelist Jim Brown made this accusation in the spring of 1986 at a revival meeting for teenagers in Ironton, Ohio, and the charge received wide publicity in the media. When we played the record backward, we could only pick up garbled and incoherent nonsense. To us it sounded like someone trying to sing in an Eastern European language while inhaling. The phrase that came the closest to comprehensible English was the reversed version of "a horse is a horse," which sounded something like "so hose isso ha."

Songwriter Jay Livingstone was not particularly troubled by the charge. When radio disk jockeys began playing the song backward to see if the message was really there, he got an unexpected boost in royalties: he's paid the same rate for his song whether it's played backward or forward.

Another curious backward-masking rumor holds that a song on a Frank Sinatra record can be played backward to reveal the telephone number of the "Florida Mafia." We haven't found the song yet, and don't believe we ever will.

★ ★ The song "Happy Birthday to You" is protected by copyright and royalties are due the songwriter every time it is sung. (1960s)

Partly true. Two sisters, Patty and Mildred Hill, wrote the song back in 1893, but with different lyrics. The original title was "Good Morning to You." In 1935 the song was republished with the familiar birthday lyrics. The Hills' original song went out of copyright back in 1949, but the lyrics to the birthday song are still protected. In fact, they will remain in copyright until the year 2010 barring any change in the copyright law.

This doesn't mean you're expected to send a check to the owner every time you sing the song at a birthday party. Royalties are due only when the song is performed, recorded, or reproduced in a commercial manner.

★ ★ If you steam the cover from the Beatles album *Yesterday and Today* you'll find a banned cover underneath—a photograph of the Beatles holding mutilated baby dolls. (1967)

True. The original cover for *Yesterday and Today* caused such an uproar when pre-released to radio stations and reviewers that Capitol Records decided to repackage the album before its general release. The first photograph showed the Beatles dressed in butchers' jackets, draped with badly damaged baby dolls and bloody cuts of meat. The replacement cover shows the boys posed around a trunk, with no controversial props. Capitol worked madly to get the records into new covers in time to fill orders, and, in their hurry, some workers simply pasted the new photograph over the old one. Just a few hundred of the pasted-over albums reached record stores, but the controversy over the picture prompted thousands of fans to deface their new albums hoping to find the banned photograph underneath. The few lucky buyers who did find the butcher cover ended up with a highly collectible item. Today the cover sells for as much as three hundred dollars.

John later claimed that the butcher picture had been a comment on America's involvement in Vietnam. Most Beatles experts consider that a pretty feeble justification. Some suggest that it was made as a comment on Capitol's cut-and-paste attitude in putting the record together out of old Beatles material.

As time went on, and more Beatles albums were released, the hoopla over the *Yesterday and*

The original cover

The replacement

Today cover mingled in people's memories with controversy and questions about other covers. Some confused the *White Album* with the pasted-over cover and assumed that its untitled, undecorated cover had been the result of hurried repackaging. In fact, the album had been left undesigned as a deliberate statement of artistic minimalism. John Lennon and Yoko Ono's album *Two Virgins* was released in 1968 with a cover photograph of the couple in the nude. It was shipped to stores inside a paper envelope, but, even so, some distributors who carried the album were arrested for dealing in pornography. That album, too, became confused with the suppressed *Yesterday and Today* cover, and, in some memories, the pasted-over Beatles photograph became a picture of the four boys in the raw. In retrospect, and in comparison to the far more shocking album covers that have been released in the years since 1967, the original *Yesterday and Today* cover seems a pretty tame subject for scandal.

★ ★ The bodies of six workers are entombed within the structure of the Hoover Dam because they fell into the cement while it was being poured. Engineers decided that to stop pouring would create a structural weakness called a cold joint, so they simply covered the men with cement. A plaque at the dam commemorates their deaths. (1940)

Not true. According to a spokesman at the Hoover Dam, engineers would not have permitted even a four-inch block of wood to be left in the cement of the dam precisely because of the danger of creating a weak spot in the structure.

The dam contains 3,250,335 cubic yards of cement, a volume greater than the largest pyramid in Egypt. It was poured in sections of roughly a thousand cubic yards at a time, each of which was allowed to cool and set before another was added. Thus, thousands of the "cold joints" of the rumor were actually part of the engineering plan.

Ninety-seven workers were killed during the construction of the dam, which was begun in 1931 and completed in 1936, but all the bodies were removed from the site for proper burial. A plaque on the finished dam does commemorate their deaths.

The rumor of the bodies in the Hoover Dam probably stems from an accident at another dam that was built at about the same time. The Fort Peck Dam, built in eastern Montana between 1933 and 1939, was at the time of its completion the largest earth-filled dam in the world. Made with one hundred million cubic yards of dredged dirt, it is even more massive than the Hoover Dam. On September 22, 1938, a huge section of the dam broke loose and slid into the lake below. Eight workers were buried in the debris, and only two of the bodies were recovered. The other six remain somewhere within the mass of the dam.

★ ★ Nine months after the blackout of 1965, the birthrate in New York City rose dramatically. (1966)

Not true. It is a common misconception that power failures, blizzards, floods, and other disasters cause a noticeable increase in the number of conceptions, and nine months later result in a surge of births. That belief is often reinforced by reports in the media.

On August 10, 1966, the *New York Times* ran a front-page story by Martin Tolchin reporting an unusual increase in the number of births at area hospitals, exactly nine months after the blackout. The writer's conclusion was based on information from several hospitals where the daily birthrate was above average. Mount Sinai Hospital logged in the most impressive numbers, with twenty-eight births on August 8, ten more than the hospital's previous one-day record. Bellevue Hospital recorded twenty-nine births on August 9, compared with an average of twenty.

On the same day fifteen babies were born at Columbia-Presbyterian, four above average, and eight were born at Coney Island Hospital, three above average. Some other city hospitals reported normal birth activity.

It was a visit to the frantic Mount Sinai Hospital on August 8, to see a friend in the maternity ward, that got the writer started. Nursing supervisor Elizabeth Brandl told Tolchin, "We've been on our toes every minute of the day, night and evening. I can't remember it ever being this bad." She speculated that the extra business must have been the result of the blackout. After checking with other hospitals, the reporter gathered some entertaining analyses from experts. Sociologist Paul Siegel told him, "The lights went out and people were left to interact with each other." Robert W. Hodge, a sociologist, explained that many people were left at home without access to their televisions. "Under the circumstances it's not unreasonable to assume that a lot of sex went on." Christopher Tietze, director of the National Committee on Maternal Health, expressed some skepticism toward the data, but guessed that "if it should be true, I would think it's because people may have had trouble finding their accustomed contraceptives."

The story made entertaining reading, but Dr. Tietze was right to question the data. An unusually high birthrate at a few hospitals does not mean that the rate for the entire city had jumped. And the two-day period studied in the article was not long enough to include all or even most of the births resulting from conceptions during the

114

blackout. J. Richard Udry conducted a more careful study of the blackout births in the August 1970 issue of *Demography*. Udry compared the daily birth figures for the entire city during the summer of 1966 with those from the previous five years. He found that the birthrate remained well within the average limits for the entire period that should have been affected by the blackout conceptions.

Though his findings clearly show that the blackout had no effect on New York City's birthrate, Udry wisely acknowledges that "a simple statistical analysis such as this [will not] lay to rest the myth of blackout babies." As we have seen time and again, rumors have little regard for the facts and many manage to thrive for years in the face of widespread denials. The blackout birth story crops up again after every major power failure and often attaches itself to any emergency condition that keeps people at home. Nine months after the Great Snow of 1967, Chicago hospitals announced that they were bracing for an onslaught of "snow babies." The expected blizzard never arrived.

★ ★ Eggs can be balanced on end only on the vernal or autumnal equinox. (1970s)

Not true. For some reason, this story has begun to appear as a regular news feature on the spring and fall equinoxes, the dates when night and day are of equal length. The story is revived every six months with newspaper and television coverage of egg-balancing parties that gather at the moment of perfect equinox. We're not sure whether subversive hoaxers are behind these parties, or whether it is a matter of mistaken belief. Eggs can be balanced on end on the equinox, if the balancer has a set of steady fingers. But they can also be balanced on end any other day of the year.

★ ★ A California woman won $3 million, the top prize in the state's roulette-wheel lottery. She was so excited that she jumped up and down with joy, causing the roulette ball to bounce into the $10,000 slot. She ended up winning the smaller prize. (1985)

True. Doris Barnett, a fifty-two-year-old Los Angeles nurse, purchased a $1 lottery ticket and won a chance to appear on television in the California lottery's "Big Spin." Her shot at the $3-million fortune was taped on December 30, 1985.

Barnett spun the wheel and watched as the ball bounced from slot to slot. When it landed in the highest prize slot, the host announced, "We have another $3-million winner," and a notice of the win flashed on the screen. Barnett jumped up and down and her family crowded onto the stage to congratulate her. In the excitement, the ball took one more bounce, landing on the $10,000 prize.

The ball had stayed in the $3-million slot for only three seconds. Lottery officials, citing a rule that requires the ball to rest in the winning slot for at least five seconds, awarded Barnett the smaller prize. Barnett has hired an attorney to challenge the decision.

Doris Barnett and "Big Spin" host Geoff Edwards, both unaware that the roulette ball has dropped from the largest prize slot to the smallest.

★ ★ During a garbage collectors' strike in New York City, one enterprising citizen got rid of his trash by putting it in a bag from a fancy store every night and leaving it on the backseat of his unlocked car. Each night the trash was stolen. (1975)

Unconfirmed. This story was widely told as one of the only light notes in the 1975 New York City garbage strike. The cunning hero very neatly pits two of the city's pressing problems—its high crime rate and the mounting piles of trash—against each other to get a positive result. It's a cheering tale of one man who overcame the city's ills. Unfortunately, it probably never happened.

The "trash in the bag" story is one in a long line of similar tales in which parcels are stolen, and the robbers end up with something unwanted, distasteful, or even dangerous. Sometimes the trick is planned, as in the trash-bag tale, and sometimes it happens by mistake. Either way the robbers get what they deserve, and the moral shines clearly through: crime doesn't pay.

In another New York City tale, a woman fed up with muggers and purse snatchers decided to take some action. One day she put a rattlesnake in her purse and walked into a neighborhood where muggers had bothered her in the past. Sure enough, a young tough grabbed her purse and ran off with it. We are left to wonder if he lived.

That story may be a direct descendant of an older legend that takes place in a rural setting.

In this one a group of boys decided to play a trick on the dishonest city slickers who often drove by on the local highway. The boys trapped a bobcat and put it in a suitcase that they set out by the side of the road. The boys hid and watched to see what would happen. Before long a car whizzed past the suitcase, screeched to a halt, and backed up. Looking furtively around, one of the passengers reached out and grabbed the bait. As the car headed off down the road, a horrible hissing and howling could be heard, and the vehicle began to swerve wildly from side to side. Obviously, someone had opened the case.

In all these stories, the criminals fall into a carefully laid trap. In other tales, the punishment is meted out by accident. One popular story concerns the theft of a dead cat. In the modern version, told since about 1970, a woman hit a cat with her car while driving through a suburban neighborhood. She found the owners by inquiring at the nearest house, and they asked her to find a way to dispose of the cat's body. It seems that their children were about to come home from school and the parents didn't want them to see the dead pet. So the woman put the cat in a shopping bag in the backseat of her car and continued on her way. She stopped to do some shopping at a local mall, and, as she was walking from the parking lot, she glanced back to see a woman opening her car and stealing the bag. She was too far away to stop the thief so she decided to go in and do her shopping. When she came out a few minutes later, there was an ambulance in the parking lot. Lying on the stretcher was the woman who had stolen the bag. Apparently she had looked at her loot and fainted. As the attendants lifted her into the ambulance, someone picked up the bag and put it on the woman's chest so that she would be sure to have it when she came to.

An older sister told us that one when we were at an impressionable age, and for a few months we believed that it had really happened to one of her friends. But before long we heard it from someone else in another part of the country who swore that it had really happened there, and we began to have our doubts. In fact, the story has been around for decades in slightly different versions. Before the era of the shopping mall, the theft took place inside a downtown department store. A woman with no yard in which to bury her dead pet was on her way to the home of a friend with a garden. She decided to stop in at the store to pick up some needed item. While shopping, she put the shoebox holding the dead cat on a counter. She only looked away for a minute, but in that time a shoplifter managed to steal the box. The woman alerted a security guard, who, acting on a hunch, found the shoplifter passed out in a ladies'-room stall, the open box on the floor beside her.

David Jacobson, in his 1948 book *The Affairs of Dame Rumor*, found this tale in wide circulation in the early 1940s, and Herb Caen, a columnist for the *San Francisco Chronicle*, wrote about it in 1938. In an even more ancient version, the dead cat is wrapped in paper and the parcel accidentally switched with a package of meat on a train or bus ride. When the cat's owners unwrap the meat they wonder with horror how the people who got the cat will react when they unwrap their package. Jan Harold Brunvand, in *The Vanishing Hitchhiker*, relates a version of this story that the teller remembers hearing in 1906. This may be the granddaddy of the many "cat-in-the-bag" stories. Curiously, it is the only version in which the victim is innocent of any wrongdoing. Apparently the moral was added as the rumor matured.

★ ★ A cookie fan called the home office of Mrs. Fields cookies and requested the recipe for the company's celebrated chocolate-chip cookie. The person who answered the phone replied that she'd be happy to send it for "two fifty," and asked the caller for her credit-card number. The woman received the recipe in the mail along with a whopping credit-card charge of $250. When the company representative had said "two fifty," she had meant $250—not $2.50. Enraged, the cookie fan sought retribution by passing out photocopies of the recipe to anyone who asked. (1985)

Not true. We heard a tamer version of the rumor in Boston in October 1985 while we were standing in line at a Mrs. Fields cookie stand to buy a half-dozen semisweet chocolate with nuts. According to the story we overheard, a disgruntled Mrs. Fields employee took the recipe with her when she left the company and offers it free to anyone who asks. A photocopied chocolate-chip cookie recipe is often brandished by the teller as the final proof that the story is true. While the complimentary recipe is usually a good one, it is not Mrs. Fields's.

The more involved version with the credit-card ingredient was reported by Bob Greene in his March 23, 1986, *Chicago Tribune* column. According to Marsha O'Shea, the Mrs. Fields spokesperson Greene consulted, the rumor is absolutely false. All Mrs. Fields employees sign an agreement with the company that they will not divulge how the cookies are made. Furthermore, the recipe is a closely guarded secret known to only three people in the company. Ms. O'Shea is baffled by the rumor. She has no idea what started it, but has seen it spread nationwide.

Though we can't say for sure, we suspect that the story grew out of an actual court case involving a chocolate-chip cookie recipe stolen from a different bakery. In 1984, a Massachusetts appellate court ruled that a former employee of Peggy Lawton Kitchens had taken the bakery's cookie recipe and used it in his own baking business. Like Mrs. Fields, Peggy Lawton Kitchens kept its recipe secret. Workers prepared the cookies from partial lists of ingredients, and care was taken to see that nobody learned the full formula. The only two copies of the complete recipe were kept under lock and key—one in an office safe and the other in a locked desk drawer. Through a pretext, the employee obtained a master key for opening the office vault, and, with a copy of the recipe in hand, he left his job to set up a competing business. Peggy Lawton Kitchens filed a lawsuit to stop him, and the court ruled that he had to stop baking the cookies. The appearance of the Mrs. Fields rumor just a year after the Peggy Lawton case was decided makes us think that news of the lawsuit may well have been the source of the rumor, distorted in retelling to make the story more interesting and dramatic.

This is one of the relatively rare "commercial vengeance" rumors, akin to the rumor (also untrue) that a celebrity who was angry at the phone company for overcharging him appeared on the "Tonight" show and gave out a credit-card number that could be used by anyone to charge long-distance calls to the phone company. Curiously, both the Mrs. Fields and "Tonight" show rumors also come with "evidence" to back them up: a working credit-card number (usually for a stolen card) with the "Tonight" show story, and a photocopied recipe with the Mrs. Fields rumor.

The cookie tale is also unusual because most rumors directed at companies that manufacture food are about disgusting foreign objects discovered by unsuspecting customers. But the Mrs. Fields story is dominated by a "flattery" element. After all, the cookie fan is motivated by her desire for cookies that are as good as Mrs. Fields's. In the "vengeful employee" version, the employee is motivated not only by a desire to limit the company's market, but also by a desire to allow everybody to make cookies that are as good as Mrs. Fields's. Of course, much of the appeal of a Mrs. Fields cookie is that you *don't* have to make it at home. Indigestible as the rumor may feel to Mrs. Fields executives, it is, after its fashion, a backhanded compliment.

★ ★ Sewers across the country flood during the halftime break on the Super Bowl. (1960s)

Unconfirmed. We thought we had the perfect test situation at hand in the 1986 Super Bowl contest between the New England Patriots and the Chicago Bears. Because the New England team had never been in a Super Bowl, interest was high in the Boston area. On top of that, some sewer systems in the area are outdated and were not designed to handle unusually high flow. We felt sure that if ever sewers would flood, this would be the time. But the game turned out to be such an overwhelming loss for the Patriots that we suspect many viewers turned off their sets in disgust before the halftime break. No sewer flooding was reported in the Boston area.

Sewer engineers we spoke with confirmed, however, that coordinated toilet flushing might cause flooding under the right conditions. Some older sewer systems were built before towns had finished growing and are consequently strained even under normal conditions. And many sewer systems are built to carry both storm runoff and sewage. In rainy weather, a town with an outgrown sewage system might very well experience some backups and flooding if many people flushed their toilets simultaneously. However, we have not been able to find any evidence that this has actually happened.

★ ★ It is against the law to kill a praying mantis. If caught in the act, you can be fined $50. (1960s)

Not true. This warning was part of the lore of our youth, and it is still widely believed. In fact, the praying mantis is a fairly common insect and is not protected under federal or state law. It is a beneficial insect, however, one that eats many crop-destroying pests, so we suggest readers continue to restrain their murderous impulses.

The only federally protected insects are ten species of butterflies, two beetles, and a moth. These are all rare bugs, and the penalties for killing any of them are quite harsh, far more severe than the rumored $50 fine for being caught with a squashed praying mantis. For knowingly killing, capturing without a permit, or selling any of these endangered insects, the penalty can go as high as $20,000 for each violation and imprisonment for up to a year. For an accidental violation, the fine can be up to $5,000. Certain state laws also protect some animals from being killed or captured within a state's boundaries, and the state penalties are generally less severe. New York, for example, lists only one protected insect, the Karner Blue butterfly. The fine for killing one is $1,000, and additional violations are fined at $250. In California, the fine for killing a protected animal is $2,000, but no insects are protected under the state's law. In Massachusetts, where we first heard the praying-mantis rumor, there are no protective laws for insects, and fines for killing other protected animals range from only $20 to $50.

A similar rumor warns that certain plants are protected by law, and that stiff fines are imposed for picking the flowers. In fact, many states do protect certain plants, but the penalties imposed are not particularly harsh. In Massachusetts, the rumored plant is the lady slipper, which, it turns out, is protected by a law passed back in 1935 that also covers wild azaleas and the cardinal flower. The fine for destroying a plant, however, is only $5, hardly enough to strike terror in the hearts of bouquet gatherers. To further dull its bite, the law only governs plants picked on state land, along state highways, or on private land without permission from the landowner. A sterner law, passed in 1920, levies a fine of up to $50 for picking a mayflower, the state flower. And for mayflowers gathered at night, the fine is $100. Presumably this second provision is aimed at true criminals.

Another commonly feared law is the one that prevents many of us from driving barefoot. The Automobile Association of America keeps tabs on driving laws in all fifty states, and reports that no such rule is on the books.

★ ★ E. L. Doctorow is actually a pseudonym for another writer or group of writers, either a committee of eight ladies (abbreviated to *E. L.*) or a black doctor whose initials are *O. W.* (*Doctor O. W.*). (1982)

Not true. Apparently the use of initials in place of a first name can create enough mystery to start a rumor these days. The E. L. actually stands for Edgar Lawrence, the name given to Doctorow when he was born in 1931.

This rumor surfaced briefly during the months of the film *Ragtime*'s first release, and it is curious because it is so easy to refute. Similar rumors about other artists, such as writers Thomas Pynchon and J. D. Salinger (*Rumor!*, page 96), and the members of the rock group Kiss (page 96), grew out of intentional secrecy and a lack of information about the subjects. But E. L. Doctorow has led a reasonably public life. He has given interviews to the press, his picture has appeared on his book jackets, and for most of his career he has held jobs that have made him easy to find—as editor-in-chief and, briefly, publisher of Dial Press, as a professor at Sarah Lawrence College, and, at the time of the rumor, as a visiting professor at New York University.

As "Eight Ladies" Doctorow, the writer of *Ragtime* would have been something like the squad of journalists who wrote the book *Naked Came the Stranger* in 1969, and the rumor may have grown in part from a memory of that book, which received wide publicity when the truth of its authorship was revealed. *Naked Came the*

Stranger was originally published as the work of Penelope Ashe, the invented name of a Long Island housewife. A real Long Island housewife named Billie Young, who in fact contributed to the writing of the book, posed as the author for radio and television appearances when the book was first published. But a month after the book's appearance the hoax was revealed. Twenty-five writers at *Newsday*, a Long Island newspaper, confessed that they had written the novel as a joke. They called it *Naked Came the Stranger* because books with "stranger" in the title seemed to sell well. And their book sold very well, particularly after news of their hoax turned it into a curiosity.

★ ★ Erich Maria Remarque, the author of the novel *All Quiet on the Western Front*, was actually named Kramer, which spelled backward is "Remark." He reversed the spelling of his name and added a French flourish in order to conceal his Jewish identity. (1940s)

Not true. Remarque was born in Germany in 1898 to Peter and Anna Maria Remarque. The antimilitary tone of his enormously successful *All Quiet on the Western Front*, first published in Germany in 1928, resulted in its censorship by the Nazis. Remarque left Germany in 1939 and became a naturalized U.S. citizen in 1947. He died in Switzerland in 1970.

★ ★ E. J. Korvette, the discount department store chain, was named for its founding by "Eight Jewish Korean War Veterans." (1960)

Not true. Eugene Ferkauf started the business in 1948, after serving four years in the U.S. Army Signal Corps during World War II. The initials *E. J.* stand for "Eugene Joe," his own first name and that of a friend and assistant in the business, Joe Zwillenberg. The name Korvette was taken from a World War II subchaser, the *Corvette*.

The chain began as a small luggage store that operated from a Manhattan loft, but it soon expanded to sell electronic appliances and other goods. In 1951 it moved to the ground floor of the same building and opened two branch stores. As the business grew, Ferkauf drew on old friends from his Brooklyn high school and from the army for management posts, and by 1960 thirty-eight of these old chums ran E. J. Korvette. These men, known inside the company as "the boys," called each other by such high school nicknames as "Doodie" and "Schmultzie." The rumor about the name probably grew from the knowledge that E. J. Korvette was an invented name and that its managers were old high school and army buddies.

The chain shortened its name to Korvettes in 1971, taking some of the steam out of the rumor, and later finished the job by going out of business completely.

★ ★ There is a secret Jewish tax on food. The tiny *K* or Ⓤ symbol on a package indicates that the manufacturer has paid the tax, which has been passed along to consumers in higher prices on the goods. (1970s)

Not true. There is no secret Jewish tax on any grocery item. This story is a plainly anti-Semitic misrepresentation of the packaging symbols that direct Jewish shoppers to goods that have been prepared in accordance with the dietary laws of the Talmud. The laws forbid religious Jews to eat certain foods, including pork, shellfish, and carnivorous animals, and prevent them from mixing meat and milk products in a single dish. Soft drinks, coffee, and sugar must be prepared under strictly sanitary conditions, and soap must contain no animal fat. The symbols on the packages indicate that the products have been inspected during preparation and conform to the standards. The *K* simply stands for "Kosher" and means that the goods have been approved by a rabbi. The Ⓤ is the more official mark of approval from the Union of Orthodox Jewish Congregations.

This rumor is based on the assumption that the rabbinical inspection is expensive enough to affect retail prices. During a radio call-in show we spoke with one Chicago woman who thought that the "secret tax" amounted to a dollar of the retail price of a package of crackers. In fact, the inspection costs do not raise prices at all. It is true that manufacturers pay a nominal fee for rabbinical inspection, but the small cost is more than offset by savings from the increased quantities of goods produced for the Jewish market.

The rumor of the secret Jewish tax is helped along by stickers that are occasionally found on grocery-store packages explaining that the *K* and ⓤ symbols mean that a "blessing fee" has been paid "to rabbis" and that the cost has been included in the retail price. Though signed "The Management," these stickers are actually distributed and applied by members of anti-Semitic groups. A letter to one such group, Truth Missions of Manhattan Beach, California, got us a supply of the stickers and a copy of an inflammatory pamphlet titled "Kosher Racket Revealed: Secret Jewish Tax on Gentiles." The pamphlet claims that the inspection program is nothing more than a racket, and that "millions upon millions of dollars have been used to line the pockets of these rabbis. The *Wall Street Journal* (April 23, 1959) called it a 20 million dollar business. . . . Today it is estimated to be in excess of 100 million dollars a year." A check of that *Wall Street Journal* article revealed that the $20 million figure referred to the total sales volume of several leading kosher food companies and had nothing to do with the cost of rabbinical inspection.

★ ★ The head of the Coors brewery in Colorado gives large amounts of money to support gun-control legislation. (1978)

Not true. W. K. Coors, chairman and chief executive officer of the Adolph Coors Company, is actually a big supporter of private handgun ownership. People who wrote the company at the height of this rumor's rampage got a letter from Mr. Coors saying, "It would be an outrageous disregard for my personal safety to support gun-control legislation. Ever since my brother was murdered 19 years ago in an abortive kidnap attempt, I have always had a gun close by for my own personal protection. I am well prepared to use it and use it effectively if need be. My personal arsenal comprises two shotguns, a hunting rifle and two handguns, and I am proficient in the use of all of them." In addition to mailing out the letters, the brewery donated money to local gun clubs and trap shoots and sponsored a documentary film with a pro-hunting stance. Because many Coors drinkers are strongly against gun control, the rumor caused the brewery a lot of headaches.

Several years earlier, when the gun-control story first started, it had been aimed at Anheuser-Busch. That company had been driven to run advertisements denying the rumor in outdoor magazines. When people wrote to Anheuser-Busch, the brewery asked them to identify the source of the story so that the firm could take legal action. They never traced the actual source of the story with these inquiries, but they may have scared some of the rumormongers into keeping quiet. Whether by the company's efforts or by the natural evolution of the rumor, Anheuser-Busch was finally freed of the story in the late 1970s, only to watch it land on Coors.

Coors, too, finally rid itself of the rumor, but a related story has since attacked yet another brewer, and it may very well be the reincarnation of the old gun-control story retold with an updated cause. In November 1983, the Stroh Brewery Company began getting calls and letters from customers in the Chicago area complaining about the company's support of Jesse Jackson's presidential campaign. The callers believed that for each case of Stroh's beer sold, the company donated a dollar to the Jackson campaign. In fact the company gave no support to Jackson, and it would have been prevented from doing so by law—a federal law prohibits corporations from giving money to any political campaign. As the customers who were spreading the rumor were also threatening to boycott Stroh products because of the alleged contributions, the company decided to act quickly to stop the story. It placed ads in Chicago papers denying that it had made any political contributions and promising legal action against anyone found responsible for starting the rumor. A $25,000 reward was offered for the identity of the story's source.

The ads brought additional publicity from the media, and the exposure served to quiet the story down. The threat of legal action may have helped shut some mouths, but the airing of the truth probably did more to silence the rumor. No takers were found for the reward offer. Damaging rumors about products and businesses are often assumed to have been started deliberately, but in fact they almost always seem to evolve naturally—from errors made when people retell stories that are already making the rounds. The Stroh's rumor was probably no exception. If it could be traced to its source, the trail would likely lead through the Coors rumor to the Anheuser-Busch rumor to stories that had been in the air long before the 1970s.

★ ★ John F. Kennedy received a salary of $1 a year while he was president. (1961)

Almost true. President Kennedy received an annual salary of $100,000 and $50,000 for expenses while he was president. However, he donated his salary to charity, a practice that he began when he entered Congress in 1947.

Kennedy did have other substantial sources of wherewithal. At the time of his inauguration, White House aides reported that President Kennedy had an annual income of about $100,000, after taxes, from trust funds established by his father. The trust funds also provided that portions of the principal be released to Kennedy and his siblings when they reached certain ages. A *New York Times* article dated April 3, 1962, reported that Kennedy had received twenty-five percent of his portion of the principal on his fortieth birthday and that he would receive another twenty-five percent, estimated at around $2.5 million, on his forty-fifth birthday.

The $1-a-year-salary story may have been based on Sargent Shriver's actual salary; Shriver, Kennedy's brother-in-law, did receive that amount annually during his tenure as director of the Peace Corps.

★ ★ Church's Fried Chicken secretly spices its food with an ingredient that makes black men sterile. The chain is owned by the Ku Klux Klan, and this is part of a plot to depopulate black neighborhoods. (1982)

Not true. Church's Fried Chicken is a publicly held company whose stock is traded on the New York Stock Exchange. The firm has no connection with the Ku Klux Klan and, in fact, has a strong record of black ownership and management of its restaurants. Food and Drug Administration tests of the chain's food have proved that it contains no harmful chemicals, and certainly none that might make men sterile.

The rumor first cropped up in New Jersey in 1982 and has since jumped in a haphazard pattern to various cities across the country. As soon as it dies down in one place, it seems to flare up somewhere else. The worst-hit cities have been San Diego (in 1984) and Memphis (in 1985). At this writing, in the spring of 1986, the rumor is very much alive in Boston. The company has a theory that the story may have come from a misinterpretation of a remark made on a television documentary about the Ku Klux Klan. The television narrator stated that Klan members "often meet in local churches." According to the theory, this was misheard by a casual listener as a reference to Church's Fried Chicken. That could be the origin of the rumor, or it could be yet another embellishment on the story.

Those who believe the rumor often think that it was reported as fact on the television show "60

Minutes" or on "Donahue." It wasn't, and the company has letters to prove it from the producers of those shows. The belief that the rumor was revealed as true on television is characteristic of many modern conspiracy rumors. It was a key element in the false rumors connecting McDonald's with protein additives and satanism in 1978 (see *Rumor!*, page 70) and in the untrue story linking Procter & Gamble to satanism in 1982 (see *Rumor!*, page 144). In those stories, the "proof" given in the telling was that a high executive in the firm had admitted the scandalous accusations on a television news show. Apparently in these weighty rumors a friend's word is not good enough, and evidence from a higher authority must now be called in to give the story credence. No executive from McDonald's or Procter & Gamble made any such admissions, and the companies' rumor battles used statements to that effect from the producers of the shows.

The Church's Fried Chicken rumor draws its surface credibility from the company's presence in poor and largely black inner-city neighborhoods. This is the result of a company policy requiring an exceptionally high return on investment. When Church's began expanding outside Texas in 1968 (the firm is based in San Antonio), it found that the higher cost of suburban locations did not allow for the targeted 21% return on capital. So, through the early 1980s, the company sought bargains in low-rent city neighborhoods. To increase profits, the company also operated for many years on a very thin marketing and advertising budget. The result of that policy is that the company does not have a well-developed public image—no friendly Colonel Sanders or Ronald McDonald comes to mind as a face behind the business. In combination, the strong visibility in black neighborhoods and the weak advertising record have left Church's vulnerable to the rumor.

New management in 1983 finally boosted the company's advertising budget and began expanding the chain into suburban areas and shopping malls. The increased advertising will eventually make Church's less of a mystery to the public, and the expansion into white neighborhoods should deflate the rumor completely. In the meantime, the company continues to deal with each outbreak of the rumor as it occurs, doing its best to emphasize that its restaurants in black neighborhoods are largely managed and staffed by members of the local black community.

★ ★ To avoid the draft, a young man had the words "fuck you" tattooed on the side of his middle finger so that it would show only if he gave a military salute. He was rejected for medical reasons. (1969)

Possibly true. This story circulated widely during the height of the Vietnam conflict, and, though it has all of the earmarks of a rumor, it also contains a kernel of truth. We haven't been able to locate the man with the tattoo, or even to find a press report that put the story forward as fact, but we have been able to ascertain that the army would have rejected him if he existed.

While draft-card burners, conscientious objectors, and the men who fled to Canada received the full glare of media attention during the era of the Vietnam draft, a much greater number avoided the draft by medical rejection. The army had no interest in training men who were likely to slow down or disrupt their units, or even those who would require special uniforms because of their size and shape. In 1970, nearly two-thirds of the men who underwent pre-induction physicals in Boston and New York were rejected for physical or psychiatric reasons.

For many young men in those years, the army's *Standards of Medical Fitness AR 40-501* was required reading. The book laid out the guidelines to be followed by doctors conducting the pre-induction physical exams and included more than four hundred physical defects considered grounds for rejection. A height of less than five feet or of more than six feet eight inches rated disqualification, as did a serious case of acne, a bad ingrown toenail, nearsightedness, asthma, homosexuality, or an allergy to bee stings. In the "Skin and Cellular Tissues" section, after listing such rejectable conditions as leprosy, elephantiasis, psoriasis, and chronic eczema, the booklet clearly states that "tattoos on any part of the body which in the opinion of the examining physician are obscene or so extensive on exposed areas as to be considered unsightly" are grounds for disqualification.

It is interesting to note that the *Standards* were revised slightly in August 1971 to narrow the tattoo loophole. The new version read, "When in the opinion of the examining physician tattoos will significantly limit effective performance of military service the individual will be referred to the AFEES Commander, for final determination of acceptability." The new wording eliminated the power of a single examiner to grant such rejections.

Also listed among the physical defects unacceptable to the army was the absence of a toe, if it interfered with normal mobility, or of more than two joints of an index, middle, or ring finger. An apocryphal tale told of a young man who chopped off a toe with an ax before going to his physical exam. According to the story, he was rejected for psychiatric reasons.

★ ★ The night J. Edgar Hoover died, President Nixon sent government troops to seize his secret files, allegedly filled with dirt on virtually every figure in American politics. The files ended up in San Clemente, and Nixon is now using them to maneuver his way back into a position of political power. (1973)

Unconfirmed but unlikely. Stories of J. Edgar Hoover's secret files began to circulate long before his death, and by 1972 the files had become almost legendary. Many assumed that Hoover had collected scandalous information on politicians for decades and used his files as blackmail to ensure large budgets and freedom of action for the FBI. But when Hoover died, on the morning of May 2, 1972, no rush was made to seize his personal files. Most of them seem to have been systematically destroyed during the weeks following his death by his longtime secretary, Helen Gandy, who apparently acted with the full knowledge of the bureau's new director, L. Patrick Gray.

During his years at the FBI, Hoover oversaw the surveillance of millions of American citizens, including many elected officials, and at the time of his death the bureau maintained over six million "official" files. All these were essentially secret, and none were accessible to the public before passage of the Freedom of Information Act in 1966. In his own office Hoover also kept a more select group of files that were closed even to those within the FBI. These were the "secret files" that caused so much concern.

In January 1975, the *Washington Post* learned from two of Hoover's former assistants that the FBI had maintained secret files on many congressmen. Their story led to a flurry of outrage in Congress and to further revelations in the press. *Time* magazine used information from "past and present FBI officials" to report that the files included information about the underworld dealings of several senators, the homosexuality of a congressman, and the reputed affairs of John and Robert Kennedy, Richard Nixon, and Eleanor Roosevelt. Another "bureau source" told *Newsweek* that Hoover kept a file on the sexual activities of a former Supreme Court justice, as well as special files on every president since Franklin D. Roosevelt.

The inevitable Senate and House investigations did not turn up much on the contents of Hoover's office files, but they did shed some light on what happened to them. Of the roughly forty-five file drawers, only two contained "official and confidential" information—considered too scandalous to be part of the main bureau files, which are available to low-level clerks. These files, 168 in all, were turned over to acting associate FBI director Mark W. Felt soon after Hoover died. Two drawers contained special bureau files that had been removed from the main stacks because of their highly confidential nature. It is not clear what became of these. The balance of the files were labeled "personal," and, according to Helen Gandy, who went through these and shredded them, they held only personal correspondence of no interest to the FBI or the public. That judgment seems questionable, as Hoover had begun to go through these files himself in the months before his death, and from the A and B drawers had removed files on such subjects as "Black Bag Jobs" and "Bombing of the U.S. Capitol"—hardly inconsequential matters. In her check of the rest of the alphabet, Gandy claims to have found nothing of importance.

The "official and confidential" files are still at the FBI, and in December 1976 the Justice Department finally released a summary of their contents with all names deleted. Many contained allegations of homosexuality or details of the heterosexual affairs of congressmen. One held information on a man who had heard rumors that Hoover himself was a homosexual.

In a democratic system, where public scandal can ruin even the most powerful elected official, compromising information can itself be a source of power. It seems clear that Hoover used his personal files to strengthen his hand in dealing with various presidents and with Congress. Such blackmail threatens the very foundation of a fair and honest democratic government, and Congress has since taken steps to curb any future abuses of the bureau's intelligence-gathering role.

Some disturbing questions do remain about the disposition of Hoover's "personal" files. We have only Helen Gandy's word that the files were destroyed and that their contents were purely personal. An anonymous letter received by Hoover's successor at the FBI, L. Patrick Gray, soon after his appointment, alleged that associate FBI director Clyde Tolson had ordered the confidential files moved to his own house on the morning of Hoover's death. That charge has been denied by those who were responsible for the files that day, and there is no evidence to support it, but since the files are gone, the suggestion of any underhanded dealings remains troubling. *Time* magazine, relying on unnamed FBI sources, also reported that the most sensitive files were removed before Gandy went through them, and that these were taken to a secret FBI hideaway in West Virginia to be burned.

While it appears unlikely that any of Hoover's confidential files ended up in the hands of Richard Nixon, it is possible that some of them survived outside the FBI's headquarters. Fortunately, as time passes and elected officials retire and leave office, any scandal the files may contain becomes less and less politically dangerous.

★ ★ A nuclear bomb accidentally exploded at Medina Air Force Base in San Antonio, Texas, in 1963. Witnesses nearby saw a huge mushroom cloud rising from the base, but the air force will not admit that the accident occurred. (1963)

Partly true. This story lingered in Texas until 1981, when the Pentagon finally admitted that a powerful explosion did occur at the base in November 1963. According to a Pentagon report made public in May 1981, 123,000 pounds of highly explosive nonnuclear material from nuclear weapons blew up in a storage facility at the base, injuring three Atomic Energy Commission employees. According to the report, there was little radioactive contamination from nuclear material stored elsewhere in the building. The exploded nonnuclear material was intended to detonate the radioactive core of nuclear weapons and had been removed from obsolete bombs being disassembled at the base.

This story demonstrates the fine line between rumor and news and shows quite clearly why people believe rumors and pass them along. They are generally dramatic stories that sound plausible, and occasionally they are based on truth. Government secrecy surrounding nuclear mishaps has created a fertile breeding ground for rumors.

Until 1981, the Pentagon admitted to only thirteen serious accidents involving nuclear weapons. Most of these mishaps (known as "broken arrows" within the military) had occurred so openly that they were impossible to conceal from the public. On March 11, 1958, for instance, a B-47 bomber accidentally dropped a nuclear bomb onto the village of Mars Bluff, near Florence, South Carolina. The nonnuclear material in the bomb detonated when it hit the ground, blasting a crater seventy-five feet across and thirty-five feet deep and completely demolishing the farmhouse of Walter Gregg. Fortunately, Gregg was working in his fields at the time with his wife and three children. Air force specialists who monitored the Greggs and their neighbors for exposure to radioactivity determined after several months that the Mars Bluff residents had escaped unharmed.

Another widely publicized accident took place on January 17, 1966, when a B-52 bomber collided with a jet tanker while refueling and crashed near Palomares, Spain. The nonnuclear material in two hydrogen bombs exploded, scattering pieces of the plutonium core over a wide area. A third bomb landed in a dry riverbed without exploding, and a fourth was found months later twelve miles offshore in the Mediterranean Sea. Because of the plutonium contamination, 1,750 tons of soil from the area were scraped into steel drums and shipped to the United States for disposal.

Another B-52 crash, on January 21, 1968, near Thule Air Force Base in Greenland, resulted in the explosion of the conventional material in four hydrogen bombs and the dispersal of plutonium over a huge area around the crash site. Over the course of four months, under the watchful eye of the international press, 237,000 cubic feet of snow, ice, and crash debris were removed to a storage site in the United States.

Press coverage and the many civilian witnesses to those incidents made government secrecy impossible. But a number of other accidents have occurred over the years on military bases or in remote locations. The Pentagon maintained a steely silence about these incidents until the release of an official accident list in 1981.

A 1950 crash and explosion at Fairfield-Suisun Air Force Base (now Travis Air Force Base) in California killed nineteen airmen and rescuers, including General Travis. It was long suspected that the blast came from a nuclear weapon, but this was not confirmed until 1981.

On June 7, 1960, a Bomarc air-defense missile at McGuire Air Force Base in New Jersey exploded in its shelter, causing a severe fire. Radioactive contamination led the air force to seal an area of about 400,000 square feet around the accident site with a layer of concrete. Officially, the air force admitted only to contamination of the destroyed launch shelter. The Pentagon's silence in this case was countered by an unconfirmed story that the problem had first been discovered by a group of officers who noticed the missile pointing into the air in launch position. According to the story, they rushed to the shelter and "yanked wires and threw switches" just in time to thwart the accidental firing. The speculation was that the near launch had been caused by the missile's reaction to radio signals from a passing police car. The Pentagon has since officially attributed the accident to the explosion of a pressurized tank of helium.

In a similar accident, on December 5, 1964, a Minuteman missile on strategic alert at Ellsworth Air Force Base, South Dakota, accidentally fired its "retrorocket" during repairs. The resulting blast caused considerable destruction, but "no detonation or radioactive damage." No details of the accident were disclosed until 1981.

The Pentagon's inventory of admitted accidents involving nuclear weapons helps to dispel much of the rumor and misinformation surrounding the mishaps, but most experts believe the official list is still far from complete. According to the records released by the Pentagon, thirty-one such accidents occurred between 1950 and 1968, and only one in the years since. It seems unlikely that the tremendous growth in our nuclear arsenal since 1968 has been accompanied by such a dramatically improved safety record.

★ ★ The Nixon administration commissioned a study by the Rand Corporation to determine the effect of canceling the 1972 presidential election. (1973)

Unconfirmed. This story was probably told as more of a cynical joke among liberals than as a genuine rumor. It probably grew out of revelations of the actual abuses of Nixon's re-election campaign, combined with a negative opinion of the Rand Corporation's contributions to the Vietnam War and the nuclear arms buildup. The Rand Corporation has conducted plenty of top-secret studies, including a strategic analysis of the hydrogen bomb that helped convince the government to go ahead with the weapon's development and a study of the strength and morale of the enemy forces in Vietnam that may have prolonged our engagement there. Because of Rand's necessarily secretive policy about its work and its close connection with the highest levels of government, the rumored election study cannot be dismissed out of hand. It seems likely, however, that, if Nixon had considered such a drastic move, some evidence of the plan would have turned up among the dirty laundry that was aired in the Watergate investigations.

★ ★ Winston Churchill, with the cooperation of officials in the U.S. government, arranged the sinking of the British liner *Lusitania* and the consequent drownings of many American passengers in order to draw the United States into World War I on the side of the Allies. (1916)

Possibly true. The *Lusitania*, at the time the world's largest ocean liner, was torpedoed by a German submarine off the south coast of Ireland on the morning of May 7, 1915, and sank in just eighteen minutes. More than twelve hundred passengers and crew members were killed. Because the casualties included many American passengers, the public outcry against the attack helped to nudge the United States from its position of neutrality and eventually led it into war against Germany in 1917.

At the time of the disaster, both the British and the American governments moved quickly to suppress evidence that the ship was anything but an unarmed passenger liner or that its sinking had been caused by anything other than German torpedoes. A British investigation tried to show that the captain of the ship was at fault for steering the liner into the path of the German submarine. In fact, the blame for the disaster must be shared by high officials in both the British and the American governments, including Winston Churchill, then first lord of the admiralty.

Colin Simpson, in his 1972 book *The Lusitania*, uncovered many long-suppressed details of the sinking that effectively disprove the official line that the attack was unexpected and unwarranted. He discovered records in the Cunard archives showing that the liner was secretly outfitted with twelve six-inch guns in September 1914. American records Simpson unearthed showed that the cargo on the final voyage of the *Lusitania* included a large quantity of explosives and ammunition—in direct violation of American law. To further compromise the ship's unarmed status, sixty-seven Canadian soldiers joined the passenger roll on the day before sailing.

For several months before the sinking, German submarines had waged an active campaign against British shipping and had tried to warn citizens of neutral countries against traveling on British boats. Yet the U.S. government had made no effort to warn its own citizens or to ensure their safety. In fact, the State Department prevented the publication of a privately placed newspaper ad that attempted to warn those sailing on the *Lusitania*. Fifty newspapers received the ad just a week before the ship's departure from New York, but only one, the *Des Moines Register*, printed it.

On the morning of May 5, as the *Lusitania* steamed toward Ireland, Winston Churchill met with Lord Fisher, admiral of the fleet, to review the situation of the navy. They were advised of the presence of a German submarine along the southern coast of Ireland and of the approach of the *Lusitania*. Instead of sending an escort ship to aid the liner Churchill and Fisher decided to order the only escort ship in the area into harbor, leaving the *Lusitania* alone and vulnerable. We will probably never know whether this decision was made carelessly or as part of a cunning strategy, but it is interesting to note that Churchill had asked Commander Joseph Kenworthy to attend the meeting. His only previous contact with Churchill had been to prepare a paper on the political repercussions of the sinking of an ocean liner with American passengers on board.

The German submarine U-20 sighted the *Lusitania* at 1:20 on the afternoon of May 7 and maneuvered to fire a torpedo at 2:10. In his log, the submarine captain recorded his surprise at the massive explosion that followed. Passengers

NOTICE!

TRAVELLERS intending to embark on the Atlantic voyage are reminded that a state of war exists between Germany and her allies and Great Britain and her allies; that the zone of war includes the waters adjacent to the British Isles; that, in accordance with formal notice given by the Imperial German Government, vessels flying the flag of Great Britain, or of any of her allies, are liable to destruction in those waters and that travellers sailing in the war zone on ships of Great Britain or her allies do so at their own risk.

IMPERIAL GERMAN EMBASSY
WASHINGTON, D. C., APRIL 22, 1915.

Warning printed in the *Des Moines Register* days before the final sailing of the *Lusitania*.

on board later testified to hearing an initial explosion from the torpedo, then, several seconds later, a second, much more powerful, explosion. The official British inquiry ruled that the liner had been sunk by two or three torpedoes, but it seems clear that the damage that caused the ship to sink so quickly came from the explosion of the cargo. Divers who have been to the wreck have reported that the bow was destroyed by a huge internal explosion, that buckled its plating from the inside.

Important information about the true nature of the *Lusitania's* cargo is still classified as secret by the United States Department of Justice and the British admiralty, and, until this is finally released, we can only speculate about what caused that devastating second explosion. But enough evidence is available to show that the *Lusitania* was not simply a passenger liner and that officials at the highest levels of government in both Britain and the United States were aware of this, yet did nothing to discourage American passengers from boarding for her final voyage.

★ ★ President Roosevelt had advance knowledge of the Japanese attack on Pearl Harbor. He did not warn the navy fleet stationed there because he hoped that the surprise attack would rally the American public behind his planned declaration of war on Japan. (1942)

Not true. Roosevelt certainly shares responsibility for the tragedy, as our country's leader and as the controlling force behind our diplomatic negotiations with Japan in the months leading up to the war, but there is no sound evidence that he withheld advance warning of the attack from the armed forces in Hawaii.

Japan's attack on Pearl Harbor, on the morning of December 7, 1941, caught the American forces completely off guard and resulted in the loss of eighteen ships, including eight battleships, and almost two hundred planes. More than two thousand servicemen were killed. The public's immediate fury against Japan gave overwhelming support to Roosevelt's declaration of war, but that same wrath was soon directed against the American leaders who seemed to have failed in their duties.

An initial military inquiry, in January 1942, pinned the blame squarely on the army and navy commanders in Honolulu, Admiral Husband E. Kimmel and Lieutenant General Walter C. Short. Both were charged with dereliction of duty for failing to take adequate defensive measures to protect the fleet and both were relieved of their posts. It may have been the severity of that ruling and its narrow focus on those two men that opened the door to speculation on who else in the government might have been at fault. Many, especially in the military, refused to accept that two seasoned military officers could alone have been responsible for such a humiliating disaster.

In fact, blame for Pearl Harbor cannot be so neatly confined to Kimmel and Short, but must more fairly be shared with a government bureaucracy that was slow and imprecise in its communications and with a wide range of strategists who did not expect the attack. Due credit must also be given to the Japanese. The attack was planned with the utmost secrecy for almost a year, and the Japanese overcame the many technical obstacles that led Americans to think the attack impossible. The Japanese force made its voyage to Hawaii in total radio silence through the virtually untraveled northwest Pacific. It accomplished a difficult refueling at sea and devised an effective way of torpedo bombing in the shallow harbor waters.

Investigations into the responsibility for our unpreparedness center on the warnings and information sent to the Hawaiian commanders by their superiors in Washington. Kimmel and Short both claimed that the warnings they had received were inadequate and that key bits of intelligence withheld from them would have led them to expect and prepare for an attack. For instance, on September 24, 1941, naval intelligence picked up a message from Tokyo to a Japanese agent in Honolulu requesting periodic information on the number and type of ships in Pearl Harbor, broken down by the area of the harbor in which they were moored. For some reason this message was not passed along to Admiral Kimmel. After the attack the message seemed a clear indication of the Japanese plans to bomb, but at the time it had been considered a routine intelligence request, similar to those made of agents in San Francisco, Panama, Portland, and other places. With the benefit of hindsight, the Hawaiian commanders were able to read this message clearly for what it was, though they had missed the point of less ambiguous warnings before the attack.

On November 27, after the breakdown of talks between the United States and Japan, both Kimmel and Short received warnings from Washington intended to alert them to possible attack. The army message read in part, "Japanese future action unpredictable but hostile action possible at any moment." The navy message began, "This dispatch is to be considered a war warning....an aggressive move by Japan is expected within the next few days." Unfortunately for Short, the army warning went on to caution against alarming the civilian population, and he took this qualification to mean that he should not increase aerial reconnaissance flights. The navy message went on to list the Philippines, Thailand, and Borneo as likely points of attack, so Kimmel was not unduly alarmed.

On December 1, Kimmel learned from his own intelligence officer that American radio surveillance had lost track of four Japanese aircraft carriers and in fact had not known their location for more than two weeks. On December 3, he was informed by the Office of Naval Operations in

157

Washington that Japanese diplomatic posts at Hong Kong, Singapore, Batavia, Manila, Washington, and London had received "urgent instructions...to destroy most of their codes and ciphers at once and to burn all other important confidential and secret documents." Navy officers in Washington considered this a clear warning of an impending Japanese military move against American and British forces within two or three days, but they did not send that interpretation with the message and Kimmel did not attach great significance to the notice. He did not even mention it to Short in their regular meeting that day, as he assumed the army had sent the same news separately. Unfortunately the army had assumed that Kimmel would pass the message on. Short later listed this information as a clear tip-off that would have spurred him to action had he received it.

Another famous missed warning has been dubbed the "winds-execute" code. On November 29, Tokyo sent the Japanese ambassador to Washington a code to listen for should normal communications channels be broken. In the event that U.S.-Japanese relations were in danger, the words "East Wind Rain" would be read in the middle of the daily Japanese-language shortwave news broadcast. Kimmel was alerted to the code that same day, and U.S. intelligence agents began to monitor Japanese broadcasts for the words from the moment the message was intercepted. They were still listening when the bombs began to fall on Pearl Harbor. Some have maintained that the execute code was sent out on December 5 and that the news was kept from the Hawaiian commanders. Even if the message had gone out, it would have been meaningless in a strategic sense. By November 29, U.S.-Japanese relations were already in grave danger, and the destruction of code machines on December 3 confirmed that.

By the morning of the December 7 attack, the Hawaiian commanders had received several warnings about the gravity of the situation in the Pacific. Through bureaucratic fumbling they did not receive some others that might have led them to take a stronger defensive position. They had not received a specific warning that Hawaii was in particular danger for the simple reason that their superiors in Washington did not know that was the case. And because the army and navy were not patrolling the waters around Hawaii, and were not carefully watching the skies with radar, the Japanese caught the fleet by surprise.

The rumor of Roosevelt's treachery does have an interesting kernel of truth. According to the story, Roosevelt lured the Japanese into the attack on Pearl Harbor so that he could declare war with popular support. In fact, Roosevelt and his cabinet were concerned that Japan make the first strike if there was to be war. At a meeting on October 16, 1941, they discussed the renewed likelihood of war created by a change in the Japanese government. As Secretary of War Henry L. Stimson recounted the meeting in his diary, "We face the delicate question of the diplomatic fencing to be done so as to make sure that Japan was put into the wrong and made the first bad move—

overt move." Again on November 25, Stimson reported that Roosevelt "brought up the event that we were likely to be attacked perhaps next Monday, for the Japs are notorious for making an attack without warning, and the question was what we should do. The question was how we should maneuver them into the position of firing the first shot without allowing too much danger to ourselves."

There the story's link with the truth ends. Roosevelt may have wanted Japan to strike first, but what could he have possibly gained for the United States by allowing an undefended strike on Pearl Harbor? What strategist would withhold intelligence in order to let the enemy destroy a major portion of his naval and air forces and kill thousands of his soldiers? The public's anger against Japan grew out of the treachery displayed in attacking without declaration of war while presenting a false front of diplomatic negotiation. If Roosevelt's aim had been to get us into war, a Japanese attack on an alerted fleet near Hawaii would have accomplished that end without the tragic and one-sided losses.

For further reading, see Gordon W. Prange, *At Dawn We Slept: The Untold Story of Pearl Harbor* (1981) and *Pearl Harbor: The Verdict of History* (1986). The first book presents a thorough summary of the events leading up to the attack and an analysis of the findings of the various boards of inquiry. The second discusses in more depth the later judgments by historians. Roberta Wohlstetter, *Pearl Harbor: Warning and Decision* (1962) is another good analysis of the subject. For an interesting presentation of the Roosevelt conspiracy theory, see John Toland, *Infamy: Pearl Harbor and Its Aftermath* (1982).

★ ★ President Roosevelt's doctors knew that he was dying before he announced plans to run for a fourth term in 1944, but they gave him a clean bill of health for political reasons. (1945)

Possibly true. President Roosevelt's personal physician, Vice Admiral Ross T. McIntire, repeatedly assured the press and the public of the president's good health throughout the 1944 campaign. McIntire continued to assert his patient's fitness until Roosevelt's death on April 12, 1945, just three months into his fourth term of office. For years the official line has been that Roosevelt's death came as a complete surprise to his doctors, but some evidence has come to light that opens that position to question.

On March 27, 1944, McIntire scheduled the president for an examination by a young heart specialist, Lieutenant Commander Howard Bruenn, at the Bethesda Naval Hospital. Bruenn's notes to McIntire and his memoranda of later presidential checkups have been closely guarded naval secrets since the president's death, but Bruenn published his own version of his findings in the April 1970 issue of the *Annals of Internal Medicine*. On his first examination of the president that day in April 1944, Bruenn found his patient tired and gray, mildly feverish, and suffering from fluid in his lungs. More critical was the condition of his heart and circulatory system. Roosevelt's blood pressure was 186/108, up from 136/78 in 1935 and 162/98 in 1937. His heart was enlarged, the pulmonary vessels were engorged, and Bruenn could hear a blowing systolic murmur, the result of excess pressure on the aortic valve.

Bruenn was concerned by his findings. To his mind, the president was in critical condition and would require rest and special care to survive even another year or two. McIntire must also have been alarmed, because he quickly called for a meeting of some of the country's leading doctors to discuss Bruenn's analysis: Frank Lahey of Boston's Lahey Clinic, James A. Paullin from Atlanta, Captains John Harper, Robert Duncan, and Charles Behrens from Bethesda, and Paul Dickens. Most of the doctors downplayed Bruenn's alarm, but Lahey and Paullin asked to examine the president for themselves at an appointment scheduled that same day. Both reported that they agreed with Bruenn's findings. Lahey thought the president should be told and put on a program of medication, while Paullin judged the situation less serious.

We may never know what McIntire told the president of his condition, but he did appoint Bruenn to attend Roosevelt on a daily basis. Apparently neither the president nor the press thought it unusual that a cardiologist had joined the White House staff. McIntire continued to issue glowing medical reports and the press continued to quote him. When the president's gray complexion, blue lips, and generally drawn appearance began to alarm the public in the fall, McIntire brushed it off as the result of dieting. "Did you ever hear of a man who recovered his flat tummy and was proud of it?" he asked at a press conference in October. To reporters' queries he flatly replied that there was "nothing wrong organically with [the president] at all. He's perfectly OK."

McIntire and many reporters ascribed the stories of failing health to political opponents and pointed out that similar stories had followed Roosevelt since his days as governor of New York, when many had said he would never survive a northern winter. His paralysis had been at the root of the stories then, and twelve years in the presidency coupled with his advancing age lent weight to the rumors in 1944. Because the rumors had been heard so many times before and because of Roosevelt's key role as the nation's leader in a time of war, few reporters probed the issue of the president's health. It was only later, after the president's death, that many looked back and wondered what information had been withheld.

Clearly McIntire had not told the nation the whole story of Roosevelt's precarious health. It is probable that he did not even tell the president. But it is less clear why he concealed Bruenn's findings. He may not have attached as much weight to Roosevelt's heart problems as Bruenn, but he must have shared some concern since he assigned Bruenn to check on the president every day. It is possible that McIntire was afraid to break the news to the president after years of presenting his own optimistic diagnoses. And it is entirely possible that McIntire kept quiet out of fear that the news would become a political bombshell.

Roosevelt died on April 12, 1945, and, at his wife's request, he was buried without an autopsy. The cause of death was officially given as a cerebral hemorrhage, though without an autopsy the finding had little meaning. McIntire died without shedding light on the mystery, and Bruenn waited until 1970 before telling his story. It is possible that one more piece of the puzzle will yet be revealed. Lahey also examined the president in April 1944, and he penned a secret memorandum about that consultation. Before his death in 1953 he gave the memo to Linda M. Strand, a friend and the business manager of the Lahey Clinic, with instructions to make it public if his role in concealing the president's sickness ever became a public issue. At this writing, Strand and the Lahey Clinic are locked in a legal dispute over ownership of the memo. There is a chance that the victor will one day make its contents known.

★ ★ Jefferson Davis was disguised in women's clothing when captured by Union soldiers at the end of the Civil War. (1865)

Partly true. Jefferson Davis, president of the Confederacy, was captured near Irwinville, Georgia, early in the morning of May 10, 1865, by a troop of federal cavalrymen. As the soldiers advanced on his camp, Davis grabbed a waterproof raglan, which turned out to be his wife's, and strode from his tent toward his horse. His wife ran after him and threw her shawl over his shoulders. Before he could get to his mount, Davis was stopped by an armed trooper. He threw down the shawl and raglan and advanced on the soldier, hoping to throw him and escape. But another party of soldiers quickly arrived and secured Davis's capture.

Though none of the official reports of the capture suggested he made any attempt at disguise, the story spread quickly through the northern states that Davis had attempted to flee in his wife's shawl and hoop skirt. Cartoonists depicted him in ridiculous women's dress attempting to run through thick brush.

In a curious way, the rumor was the North's revenge for an earlier story. At the time of Abraham Lincoln's inauguration, tension was high between pro- and anti-slavery factions in the country, and many feared for the president-elect's safety when he arrived in Washington. On the advice of those responsible for his security, Lincoln slipped into the city unannounced some days before the inauguration. As a result of this attempt at secrecy, a peculiar story spread through the South that Lincoln had come to the capital disguised in a long robe and a Scottish tam-o'-shanter.

More than a hundred years earlier, the defeated leader of another rebellion actually did make his escape disguised in women's clothing, and his memory may have given rise to the rumor about Jefferson Davis. Prince Charles Edward

Prince Charles Edward Stuart disguised as Betty Burke   Pilgrim Press, Derby, England

Stuart, better known as Bonnie Prince Charlie, leader of the 1745 Jacobite Uprising in Scotland, spent many weeks evading capture after his forces were defeated at Culloden. Before he was finally able to escape by ship to France, he roamed through Scotland's western islands, protected by a small band of loyal supporters. On one occasion he fled from the Isle of Skye disguised as an Irish girl named Betty Burke. Those who accompanied him later admitted that his long stride was far from ladylike and that he continually fussed with his headdress.

★★ German soldiers cut off the hands of hundreds of Belgian babies during World War I. (1914)

Not true. Though this atrocity was never committed, it has come down through the decades as a common piece of misinformation about World War I. The story was first reported by the Paris correspondent for the London *Times* on August 27, 1914, who wrote:

> One man whom I did not see told an official of the Catholic Society that he had seen with his own eyes German soldiery chop off the arms of a baby which clung to its mother's skirts.

The report is decidedly thin on verification and reads suspiciously like a rumor heard through a friend of a friend, but it served the purpose of inflaming public opinion against the Germans, and no official corrections followed it into print. A few days later, the same correspondent turned the incident into a methodical German policy: "They cut the hands off the little boys so that there shall be no more soldiers for France." Over the next few months, the mutilated babies grew in number and gradually moved from France to Belgium while Allied officials sat back and watched the story gather momentum. Occasionally the Allies gave the story a helpful nudge to make sure it stayed alive and well. Propaganda photographs were manufactured to show groups of the handless children. As the war went on, these became more and more lurid, showing German soldiers eating the severed hands, or the Kaiser himself with a butcher's knife and a chopping block surrounded by piles of little hands.

From the 1914 rumor of a single German atrocity, the stories grew more and more elaborate. On May 2, 1915, the London *Sunday Chronicle* printed a pathetic version of the tale:

Some days ago a charitable great lady was visiting a building in Paris where have been housed for several months a number of Belgian refugees. During her visit she noticed a child, a girl of ten, who, though the room was hot rather than otherwise, kept her hands in a pitiful little worn muff. Suddenly the child said to the mother: "Mamma, please blow my nose for me." "Shocking," said the charitable lady, half-laughing, half-severe, "a big girl like you who can't use her own handkerchief." The child said nothing, and the mother spoke in a dull, matter-of-fact tone. "She has not any hands now, ma'am," she said.

The grand dame looked, shuddered, understood.

"Can it be," she said, "that the Germans—?" The mother burst into tears. That was her answer.

When the United States finally entered the war in 1917, the stories were twisted to appeal to American sentiments. An American couple was rumored to have applied to adopt two orphaned Belgian children. When they arrived from Europe, the children turned out to be handless. One

World War I propaganda cartoon of handless Belgian child   New York Public Library

Iowa paper assigned a photographer to get a picture of the children, who were said to be in the Des Moines area. A search revealed that the unfortunates had been invented by an energetic Liberty Bond salesman.

A few reporters made efforts to get at the truth of the story during the war, but their findings were largely ignored. United Press correspondent William G. Shepherd wrote in the March 1917 *Everybody's Magazine*:

> I was in Belgium when the first atrocity stories went out. I hunted and hunted for atrocities during the first days of the atrocity scare. I couldn't find atrocities. I couldn't find people who had seen them. I traveled on trains with Belgians who had fled the German lines and I spent much time among Belgian refugees. I offered sums of money for photographs of children whose hands had been cut off or who had been wounded or injured in other ways. I never found a first-hand Belgian atrocity story; and when I ran down second-hand stories they all petered out.

After the war, more people came forward to refute the mutilation stories. Italian prime minister Nitti wrote that his government, in cooperation with the British, had looked into the truth of every atrocity accusation that came to them, in particular the reports of handless Belgian children. He found that "every case investigated proved to be a myth." Nitti also wrote of a rich American who sent a representative to Belgium after the war with money to set up the handless Belgian youth in some sort of useful jobs. He was unable to find a single mutilated child.

★ ★ The Red Cross makes millions of dollars by selling donated clothing and supplies to U.S. soldiers stationed overseas. (1917 and 1942)

Not true. This story reared its head in World War I and again in World War II to discredit the entirely humanitarian efforts of the American Red Cross. During both wars the Red Cross called on volunteers to knit socks and sweaters and to make bandages to be sent to American servicemen fighting abroad. The rumor of Red Cross profits made these volunteer knitters feel that they had been cheated, and many of them stopped contributing to the program in disgust. Of course the story was untrue, but, by the time denials reached the knitters, much damage had already been done.

One 1942 elaboration on the story told of a woman who had embroidered her name and address inside the sweater she made for the Red Cross. Weeks later she received a letter from a sailor thanking her for the sweater but wondering if she knew that the Red Cross had charged him $6 for the garment. Soldiers in Iceland were rumored to be paying $7.50 for their Red Cross sweaters, while men in the Pacific were said to pay $5. One knitter was said to have found her sweater on sale in a local department store; the presumption was that the Red Cross had sold it. Another story alleged that the donated sweaters were shredded in England and the wool sold at premium rates. None of these stories was true, but they had the very real effect of discouraging volunteers from contributing to the Red Cross programs.

Similar rumors plagued the Red Cross blood drives during World War II. Much of the blood was said to be wasted because the supervisors of the program carelessly accepted diseased donors without first testing them. When problems were later discovered, quantities of blood had to be destroyed. Another story charged that much of the blood was wasted because it could not be kept for more than a couple of months. And other rumors revealed deep-rooted racism and ignorance—that white servicemen given blood from Asian or black donors now stood a good chance of fathering children with characteristics of those races. The stories were groundless, but again they interfered with the worthy efforts of the Red Cross.

Stories like these were often reinforced by enemy propaganda coming into the country on short-wave radio programs. The programs built up an audience by broadcasting information of great interest to Americans, such as interviews with American prisoners of war, and balanced this with a good measure of false or distorted news. During both World Wars, propaganda from both sides of the battle line contributed to a wealth of rumor around the world.

★★ German tanks operating in North Africa during World War II maintained a decisive edge over the Allied forces because the German tanks were air conditioned. (1944)

Not true. Rommel's tank forces did maneuver successfully against the Allies in North Africa, but it was not because the tanks were air conditioned. A similar rumor among the British forces held that the American tanks were air conditioned, and the story inspired no small amount of jealous hostility. All the tank soldiers on both sides had to endure the stifling heat of their closed machines. Even today tanks are not built with air conditioning. The Germans won battles through the tactical use of leapfrogging batteries of anti-tank guns.

Another peculiar rumor from the North African front told of mutually agreed-upon cooling-off breaks. American soldiers training in the U.S. believed that German and British officers arranged frequent truces so that the tank operators could get out of their sizzling machines and stretch. According to the story, soldiers from both sides sat and smoked together during these short breaks, before climbing back into their tanks to resume the battle. Rommel was also rumored to be a regular dinner guest of the British officers. The army did its best to bring the soldiers' image of the war back to reality. A spokesman at the Fort Knox training center announced, "It is illogical that well-trained troops would take the risk of so trusting each other and senseless that Rommel, particularly, would so risk his neck."

★ ★ American flyers who crashed in a remote area of China during World War II were taken prisoner by a semicivilized tribe called the Lolos and made to live as slaves. (1946)

Not true. This story apparently spread from American forces in China at the end of the war and caused enough concern among the public back home that the army conducted a full-fledged investigation. After months of negotiation, American officials were allowed to enter the area and meet with Lolo chieftains. Expecting the savages of the rumor, the Americans were surprised to find the Lolos quite cooperative. The Chinese allowed the officials to make a thorough search of the entire area, but not a single American flyer was found.

The incident cost taxpayers thousands of dollars and diverted manpower from important military projects. It stands as yet another example of the power of rumor. It also has a disturbing parallel in the undying American concern over the soldiers still listed as missing in action from the war in Vietnam. Until the Vietnamese cooperate as the Chinese did in the Lolo incident, the lingering hope that some of these soldiers remain alive will continue to haunt the families and friends of the missing.

★ ★ The handgrip of the M16 rifle was made by Mattel. When the gun was first introduced in Vietnam, soldiers noticed the toy company's logo embossed on the handgrip and complained. Later shipments arrived without the imprint, but the grips were still made by Mattel. (1969)

Not true. The Colt Patent Firearms Manufacturing Company made the M16 rifle during the Vietnam era and still does. Mattel never had any part in the manufacture of the gun and never supplied parts. Mattel has never even made a toy M16 and makes no toy guns today. The toy company did make a "burp gun" in 1956 and a toy reproduction of the Springfield rifle in about 1965, but we doubt that these had anything to do with the rumor. The story probably grew out of the public controversy over the M16, centering on its early problems with jamming.

The M16 was designed as an automatic lightweight rifle that operated on the principle that spray fire was more effective in combat than carefully aimed shots. Its first combat test came in Vietnam in 1962, and it received glowing reports. But before placing any large orders, the army made some small changes in the design that ended up causing a host of problems. Soldiers began receiving the guns in quantity in 1964, and the first thing they noticed was the rifle's light weight. Because it used a smaller bullet with a less powerful charge, the M16 was much lighter than the M1 and M14 rifles it replaced. Any change is likely to draw criticism, and some soldiers undoubtedly felt that a lighter rifle would also be less reliable and less effective in combat. The later rumors may have been based on these uninformed gut reactions. In fact, the rifle performed amazingly well during its first months in combat.

Late in 1966, however, at about the time the army selected the rifle as the standard U.S. combat weapon, soldiers began to report serious problems. In the jungle combat conditions of Vietnam the rifle had a tendency to jam. The controversy eventually reached the level of congressional hearings, and the problems were traced to design changes made by the army, to a change in the type of powder used in the gun's ammunition, and to lack of proper care in the field. The faults were corrected, but to the soldier in Vietnam the gun had earned an image of unreliability. The false story of the Mattel handgrip is one expression of the soldiers' feelings about the rifle.

★★ Jockey shorts make men sterile. (1940s)

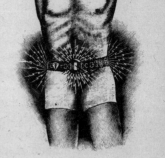

Not true. This old husband's tale has dogged Jockey shorts since they were introduced in the 1930s. Inspired by the close-fitting bathing suits then in style on the French Riviera, the shorts proved an immediate success in America. But from the beginning people whispered that the shorts somehow made men sterile.

The belief seems to have come from scientific experiments showing that a man's testicles produce more sperm when kept cold. One study (using prisoners at Oklahoma State Prison) compared the sperm counts of men whose testicles had been chilled with ice to those of men whose testicles had been heated with heat lamps. The chilled testicles produced an above-average count, while the count from the heated testicles was below average. From these results some concluded that tight-fitting briefs, which hold the testicles closer to the body than boxer shorts, must also keep them warmer and thus make a man sterile. That's a big assumption, and one that has not been borne out by any of several experiments using actual Jockey shorts. Even heated underwear would not make a man sterile;

177

it would merely lower his sperm count and make him slightly less fertile.

Despite the lack of conclusive data, many doctors advise male patients with fertility problems to switch from briefs to boxer shorts. Stories in the press also reinforce the Jockey-short fears from time to time. "Dear Abby" has periodically run letters from readers who have solved their fertility problems by changing the style of their underwear.

The makers of Jockey shorts don't seem to be too concerned with the rumor these days, though the story is still circulating. Sales of Jockey-style briefs have been steadily gaining on the boxers and today account for almost eighty percent of the men's underwear market. And in the fifty years since their introduction, Jockey shorts have been worn by an awful lot of fathers.

★ ★ It is dangerous to pop pimples in certain places on your face because it may lead to brain infection.

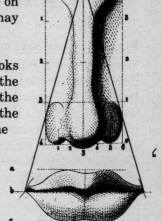

True. Anatomy textbooks have long warned about "the danger triangle" on the face—the area between the bridge of the nose and the corners of the mouth, because the blood there drains into the cavernous sinus at the base of the skull. Blood flow in the cavernous sinus is slow, and an infection there can be hard to get rid of, even with modern antibiotics. Admittedly, the danger triangle was of more concern in the days before antibiotics, but it continues to be an attention getter in high school health classes, and it is still mentioned in many medical textbooks. Bernard Leibgott's *The Anatomical Basis of Dentistry*, published in 1982, contains this warning: "Facial infections, furuncles, pimples, and so on should not be poked or squeezed for fear of sending infective material to the cavernous venous sinus."

★ ★ If you can tear the label off a Michelob bottle straight through the letter "i" you will have good luck. (1970s)

Unconfirmed. Such an ability is probably just a sign of a misspent youth. This rumor is closely related to the "virgin indicator" rumors discussed in *Rumor!* (page 45)—that if you can peel the foil from a gum wrapper in one piece, or if you can peel the label from a beer bottle in one piece, you are a virgin. These rumors seem to circulate widely in restaurants while people are waiting for the pizza to bake.

★ ★ A man chewing tobacco came to a particularly tough and chewy chunk in his wad. He chewed for some time, and finally took the tobacco out of his mouth to discover he'd been chewing on part of a dried human thumb. (1918)

Partly true. This story has circulated for decades, often told with the chewer as a distant friend or relative. We first heard it from a grandparent in southern Ohio who swore it had happened to his father-in-law. It sounds too revolting to have any basis in fact, but a very similar case actually came to court in 1918. Bryson Pillars, of Hinds County, Mississippi, bought a package of Brown Mule chewing tobacco and began to chew it plug by plug. The first one was fine, according to the court records, "but when the appellant tackled the second plug it made him sick, but, not suspecting the tobacco, he tried another chew, and still another...while he was getting 'sicker and sicker.' Finally, his teeth struck something hard; he could not bite through it. After an examination he discovered a human toe." The record tactfully refrained from listing the "further harrowing and nauseating details."

The Supreme Court of Mississippi ruled that Pillars had suffered from ptomaine poisoning as a result of his bout with the Brown Mule, and ordered the R. J. Reynolds Tobacco Company to pay damages. As part of its decision, the court stated, "We can imagine no reason why, with ordinary care, human toes could not be left out of tobacco, and if toes are found in chewing tobacco, it seems to us that somebody has been very careless."

It is curious that the legend, as we have heard it, makes no mention of sickness, ptomaine poisoning, or even a lawsuit, but ends with the chewer discovering the thumb. The story is probably based on the Pillars case or another similar one and has been refined through retelling.

The story is very similar to that of the mouse found in the soft-drink bottle (see *Rumor!*, page 53), in which a woman at a soda counter finishes her drink only to find a decomposed mouse at the bottom. That story is also based on at least one actual incident, but has evolved into a legend that varies little from telling to telling and almost always ends in a lawsuit. Because such contaminations are extremely rare, the story is generally told by people who have no connection with an actual victim. But in classic rumor form the tale is related as if it had happened to a friend of a friend of a friend.

Another gruesome story, along the same lines, tells of a diner in a fine restaurant who finds a thumb floating in his soup. It turns out that one of the chefs had an advanced case of leprosy. Fortunately, we have been able to find no factual basis for this one, and we are happy to leave it in the realm of fiction.

★ ★ A worker drowned in a vat of beer at the Lone Star brewery in San Antonio. (1966)

Not true. The incident never happened. The rumor spread through Texas in the winter of 1966 and 1967, and one of our sources even heard it mentioned on the radio. In some versions the worker had been murdered and his hands cut off so he couldn't swim or escape. The story never grew into major rumor proportions and didn't cause the brewery undue concern, but it is of interest as a reappearance of an old and enduring contamination legend. Over the years it has been told about vats of soft drinks, hard liquor, tomato juice, and various sauces. Though Lone Star was happily rid of the tale by 1967, the story has since resurfaced in slightly different form.

Rumors like this tend to leap from company to company as they change. While evolving, they tend to attach themselves to ever bigger firms and ever more popular products, probably for the simple reason that a shocking story makes better telling when a well-known name is involved. So it is not surprising that this rumor eventually placed the dead worker in a vat of Coca-Cola. (Again, of course, the story was completely fictitious.) The soft-drink company has been the target of occasional versions of the rumor for at least thirty years, though the legend rarely spread far enough to cause a loss of business. In 1981, however, the story created serious problems in the Far East. For some reason, the tale caught the public's attention in one major city that summer, and within a month had created such concern among consumers that sales of Coca-Cola began to drop. To prevent sales from sliding further, an industry association issued an official press release denying the story and even took out ads in local newspapers to explain the truth.

Once again the story fizzled out, but we will be surprised if we've heard the last of it. The legend has been around for decades, and it is almost certain to reappear from time to time— told about different products and with new and more shocking embellishments.

One old variant that may be the ancestor of the modern rumor tells of a corpse discovered in a half-consumed barrel of alcohol. In the eighteenth and early ninteenth centuries when a person of wealth and rank died far from home the remains were sometimes shipped back for burial preserved in a cask of alcohol. Admiral Horatio Nelson was perhaps the most famous of these pickled corpses. He was killed at the battle of Trafalgar in 1805 and his body shipped back to England in a barrel of brandy. According to the legend that later arose, when the barrel was finally opened, it was found to be drained of its liquor; sailors on the ship, unaware of the true contents of the barrel, had tapped it for some illicit tippling. The expression "tapping the admiral" was used by British sailors in the nineteenth century to describe an unauthorized drink from a cask by means of a straw, and is a clear reference to the legend of Nelson's lost brandy. Similar stories told of barrels switched in transit or discovered in old houses. In the legends the body was always found after most of the liquor had been drunk.

Even older legends concern bodies preserved in vats of honey. Alexander the Great was said to have been embalmed in honey, his body displayed under glass in Alexandria so that mourners could see his face beneath the syrup. The Arab historian Abd el Latif wrote in the thirteenth century of a group of treasure hunters who found an ancient sealed jar of honey while exploring the tombs beneath the Egyptian pyramids. They settled down to a delicious lunch, dipping their bread into the jar, until one of the diners pulled out a human hair. A quick investigation revealed the preserved body of a child curled up at the bottom of the jar. The historian credits the story to "an

Egyptian worthy of belief." If he had checked further, we suspect he would have encountered the familiar chain of friends of friends of friends.

★ ★ A little girl became separated from her mother while they were shopping at a department store. The mother notified the security guards, who discovered the child in the men's room, dressed in boys' clothing, her head shaved, apparently about to be kidnapped. (1984)

Not true. Rick Baker wrote about this rumor for the *Peoria Journal Star* on May 23, 1984, after people in the area had worked themselves into a frenzy worrying about the safety of their children. He interviewed police detectives and store managers to find out if there was any truth to the story and found that there wasn't. Not a hair. The police first heard the story when they got a call from City Hall in March asking them to look into it. Their investigation turned up only friends of friends of friends in classic rumor fashion, and they finally gave up the chase.

Baker found that the story was widespread not only in Peoria, but in other Illinois cities, including Galesburg and Bloomington. Within a few weeks it had spread well beyond the Illinois borders and was plaguing police departments and department-store managers in New Orleans and

Boston. On November 21, Ann Landers gave it a massive boost when she printed a letter detailing the story and signed "West Coast Warning." Landers replied, "Dear West Coast: Your letter is a somber reminder of what can happen if a child is allowed to wander off for even a moment. Thanks for the alert." Landers captured the moral of the story perfectly, though she really should have checked for facts before giving the rumor such wide play.

If the many journalists and detectives who have tried to track this rumor down had instead done some reading in folklore and rumor studies, they would have found that the story has been around, with some variations, for decades. Elements of the story go back hundreds of years. In the 1970s, the most common version told of a teenage girl who was abducted from the restroom at a mall or department store after being injected with sedatives. According to the rumor, the girl was kidnapped for a life of white slavery in New York City or South America. Often the story had the victim rescued at the last minute as she was being dragged to the parking lot by thugs. In the 1960s, the story told of a young boy who went into a men's room while his mother continued to shop. When he didn't come out, she went in and found him covered with blood, his penis cut off. A gang of teenagers was later found to have the penis; it had been cut off as a gang initiation rite. This rumor was often told with a racial slant; if the child was black his butchers were white, or if he was white the teenagers in the gang were black.

David Jacobson, in his 1948 book *The Affairs of Dame Rumor*, discussed the child-mutilation rumor as it was told in the forties and pointed out that it had an extraordinarily long history. Similar stories with anti-Semitic overtones have been told for centuries; these describe the kidnap of Christian children for ritual sacrifice. Folklorist Bill Ellis has found an even older version of the story told as an anti-Christian rumor. In the second and third centuries it was said that Christians, as part of an initiation rite, regularly murdered Jewish children.

━━━━━━━━━━━━━━━━━━━━━━━━━━━━━━━━

★★ Two Union Pacific Railroad welders were killed when sparks ignited disposable butane lighters in their pockets. The lighters exploded with the force of three sticks of dynamite. (1979)

Not true. No worker at the Union Pacific Railroad has ever been injured in an accident of this sort. And, according to the Federal Railroad Administration, the Interstate Commerce Commission, and the Association of American Railroads, no such accident has occurred on any American railroad. The Consumer Products Safety Commission reports that there is no real danger of explosion from disposable butane lighters, and they have not heard of any accidents involving the lighters as serious as the one described in the rumor.

This is a good example of a modern photocopy rumor—one that has been widely disseminated through duplicated health bulletins sent out or posted by union and railroad company officials. The story probably began as an old-fashioned word-of-mouth rumor, but it was soon picked up by worried officials and spread further with the help of copy machines. A typical example is the report issued by the Topeka office of the Santa Fe Railroad on July 25, 1979:

> Group 6 Welders & Welder Helpers:
> Recently on a neighboring railroad, two Mechanical employees were killed as a result of butane cigarette lighters exploding. In both cases the men were involved in welding or burning, and sparks penetrated the plastic housing of the lighter, causing the liquid butane to explode with *the equivalent of three sticks of dynamite.*
> Therefore, all employees involved in welding, cutting and grinding operations should immediately discontinue use of liquid butane lighters while on duty.

By November 1979, the Union Pacific Railroad was fed up with the story. The company had fielded hundreds of calls from reporters and from worried safety directors at businesses around the country. Two major newspapers had printed the rumor as fact, and Paul Harvey had mentioned it on his syndicated radio program. So the railroad issued a press release categorically denying the story. Union Pacific's safety director was quoted as saying, "It just didn't happen. Union Pacific certainly doesn't endorse butane lighters, or any other product, for that matter. But we are deeply concerned when our name is used in such a reckless story."

For the rumor researcher, the most telling part of Union Pacific's press release described the company's search for the story's origin: "Extensive research by Union Pacific has failed to turn up an original source for the story. In each case it was based on hearsay and personal opinion." A classic rumor. We wonder how many hours have been spent in fruitless searches for the starting point of rumors. Reporters and company officials, used to dealing with facts and verifiable statements, generally assume that somebody must have deliberately made these stories up and that a thorough search will eventually ferret the person out. But there never seems to be such a person.

The butane-lighter story continued for several more months, appearing in a few more publications (such as the January 1980 issue of *Forestry News*) and circulating in photocopied warnings. Herb Caen of the *San Francisco Chronicle* wrote of receiving one of the lighter warnings on U.S. Department of Transportation stationery in December 1980. He refuted it in his column with a quote from a Union Pacific spokesman. Since then the tale seems to have petered out.

In the spring of 1980, the rumor briefly attached itself to comedian Richard Pryor. When the news of his serious burns first reached the public, many believed that he had been hurt by an exploding butane lighter. He had not. As he later admitted, the burns were caused by a drug-related accident. Pryor's near-fatal mishap should indeed be taken as a warning about the dangers of drug abuse, but it should not scare anyone away from buying butane lighters. Disposable butane lighters don't explode.

───────────────────────────────

★ ★ A welder wearing soft contact lenses suffered a gruesome accident. The spark of his welding torch generated microwaves that fused the lenses to his eyes. Not realizing what had happened, he removed the lenses at the end of the day and pulled the corneas from his eyes. He is now totally blind. (1983)

Not true. Like the rumor of the exploding butane lighter, this tale spread quickly through the country on the wings of photocopied health bulletins. And, like the earlier rumor, it is completely untrue. Not only did the accident never occur, but medical experts have confirmed that the accident couldn't happen as described—that contact lenses cannot "fuse" to a person's eyes.

The American Academy of Ophthalmology has looked into the matter and found the story bogus. According to the academy, "exposure to electric arc welding is not associated with an increased risk of ocular damage in individuals who wear contact lenses." The academy's doctors warn, however, that any worker exposed to electric arc welding should take the usual precaution of wearing protective goggles.

The story of the blinded worker spread by word of mouth and by photocopy during the early part of 1983, frequently naming the United Parcel Service or Duquesne Light Company, of Pittsburgh, as the company where the accident took place. Neither company, of course, had anything to do with the rumored injury. On April 4, 1983, an Associated Press report delved into the rumor and followed it back to a warning posted in February at the Genstar Stone Products Company in Hunt Valley, Maryland. Genstar's safety director got his information in a letter from another company, but the AP reporter dropped the trail there. The American Academy of Ophthalmology followed it back further and may have found its source in an actual, though somewhat different, accident. In 1967 a welder at a Bethlehem Steel plant in Baltimore who wore both contact lenses and safety glasses was injured when an electrical switch box exploded. The worker had worn his contacts for at least twelve hours before arriving for work, and that overuse, coupled with the force of the explosion, caused abrasions to his corneas. According to the academy, "the contact lenses did not fuse to the cornea and the vision returned to normal within several days. The two ophthalmologists who treated the worker reported that the electrical flash had no part in causing the injury."

It is quite possible that the relatively minor injury to the Bethlehem Steel worker in 1967 was the source of the greatly distorted stories of 1983.

But the ophthalmologists' press releases did little to slow the rumor. The *Chicago Tribune* published an exposé of the tale on April 4, 1983, quoting Frank Wondrasch, national safety director for United Parcel Service, as saying, "It never happened. But I must have talked to every corporate safety director in the country."

★ ★ A woman bought a new dress at a large department store downtown. The first night she wore it, she noticed a strange smell. As the evening wore on, she began to feel sick. Then she fell over and died. It turned out that the store had bought some surplus shrouds from an undertaker and had made them into dresses. Formaldehyde fumes lingering in the cloth had killed the woman. (1930s)

Not true. A caller to a radio show in New York City told us this story as a rumor she had heard in her youth. As she had heard it, the victim was a friend of her mother who had bought the dress at Klein's department store on Fourteenth Street in the days when that was a fashionable shopping thoroughfare. Folklorists have found much the same story in circulation in the Midwest in the 1940s; there the victim succumbed to the fumes while dancing at a party. In that version, the dress itself had been worn by a corpse and then returned to the store for resale. Again, it was formaldehyde that killed the dress's second owner. The name of the store varied with the telling, but it was generally one of the biggest in a given area. The story is still told from time to time, and either formaldehyde or embalming fluid always kills the alleged victim.

The rumor seems to be an old one and may have been around long before Klein's department store was built. Jan Harold Brunvand discusses the story in his book *The Choking Doberman*, and points out the close parallel to the Greek myth of Hercules, who died when his wife, Dejanira, secretly wet his shirt with the blood of the centaur Nessus. Hercules had killed Nessus, but the dying centaur had convinced Dejanira to save a vial of its blood for use as a love potion. Some time later, Dejanira felt jealous of another woman and soaked Hercules's shirt in the blood, taking care to wash out any visible stain. Hercules wore the shirt, and as his skin warmed it, the poison worked its way into his body. He tried to tear the garment off, but hunks of his own flesh came off with it. In agony, he burned himself on a funeral pyre.

★ ★ A woman trying on a fur coat at a downtown department store felt a sharp prick on her arm. When a salesclerk helped her take off the coat, a baby cobra was discovered in the sleeve. The woman was rushed to a hospital, where her life was barely saved. A check of the rest of the shipment of coats, which had come from Southeast Asia, turned up dozens of the baby snakes. A nest of cobra eggs had apparently hatched in the shipment during the long ocean voyage. The woman was paid to keep the incident quiet out of fear of a panic that might hurt both the store and the downtown business district. (1969)

Not true. It is conceivable that a single incident may have provided the seed for this rumor, but so far none of the many researchers who have tackled the story has discovered one. The story has attached itself falsely to virtually every major department store in the country. In various versions the snakes are found hiding in rugs, blankets, sweaters, and fruit. Often the customer dies.

When the rumor first cropped up, journalists in many cities took up the hunt, trying to find the actual victim or the doctor who had treated her. But after tracking the story through friends of friends of friends and watching it change from cobras to asps and from coats to shirts to rugs as the chain was followed, most researchers realized that they were dealing with a modern myth.

A similar rumor of a poisonous snake attack scared many people away from Montreal's Botanical Garden in the summer of 1983. The park has long been a popular spot for wedding photographs when the flowers are in bloom, and the rumor that summer told of a bride who was bitten by a poisonous viper that had been lurking in the foliage. Garden officials and wedding photographers did their best to set the record straight, pointing out that no poisonous snakes live in Canada, but many wedding parties sought less worrisome backdrops for their pictures anyway. While the snake-in-the-coat story seems to draw on Freudian imagery and lurking subconscious fears, Montreal's wedding snake is closer to a modern retelling of the story of Adam and Eve.

Curiously, in the summer of 1985 the Ford Motor Company encountered a real-life problem not unlike the snake-in-the-coat rumor. According to an Associated Press story (printed in the *Detroit Free Press* on July 24, 1985), a worker at Ford's Saline, Michigan, assembly plant discovered a black widow spider hidden in a plastic dashboard part imported from Mexico. During the month of July more than two dozen other spiders were flushed out of the parts at the Ford factory, while efforts were made in Mexico to spiderproof the plastics plant. A three-foot-wide band of insecticide was laid down around the Mexican building, and all the dashboard parts were dipped in insecticide before being shipped.

By the end of July, Ford seemed to have the problem licked, but not before the UAW had brought the issue up in collective bargaining. Thanks to the spiders, at least some of the plastic dashboard parts are now being made in Michigan, while imports from Mexico have been reduced.

★ ★ A man answered an ad in the paper for an "almost new" Porsche on sale for $50. He assumed the paper had misprinted the price, but, when he arrived at the address, a woman answered the door and assured him that indeed $50 was all she was asking. He then went into the garage to see the car, expecting some sort of wreck. But it was in perfect condition—less than a year old and without a scratch. He paid up on the spot. As he was getting ready to leave, he asked the woman why she was selling the car. She explained that her husband had run off with his secretary and had written from New York City instructing her to sell the car and the house and send him the money. (1979)

Not true. Ann Landers reported a version of this tale as fact in 1979, faithfully swallowing the story as sent by one of her readers, who claimed to have read it in the *Chicago Tribune*. Landers even had the *Tribune*'s managing editor check on the story, only to find that "his researchers could not find it in their paper." That didn't stop her from flatly declaring that "the incident did happen as reported and was a news story somewhere." Where? we ask.

The story makes for great telling, and is always good for a laugh, but it is fiction from start to finish. Folklorist Stewart Sanderson has traced it to a similar tale told in Britain since 1948, in which the woman sells the car as instructed by her late husband's will, which specified that she send the money to his mistress.

A similar tale about a late-model car on sale for a low price ends with the news that the previous owner had died in the car. His body had not been discovered for several months, and, though the car looked great and ran perfectly, the smell could not be removed.

This one, too, has been around since the 1940s and crops up periodically as a fresh rumor about a supposedly recent occurrence. One folklore researcher who delved into the history of the legend came up with what he suspects is its factual basis. Richard M. Dorson traced the story back to Michigan in the early 1940s, where it made the rounds as an anonymous rumor, then to the small black community of Mecosta, in the center of the state, where he came across a firsthand account of an actual event in 1938. In Dorson's apparently true story, a man committed suicide in a custom-decorated 1928 Ford and was not discovered for three months. It is entirely possible that that 1928 Ford is the kernel of truth behind the modern tale of the $50 "death Porsche."

★ ★ A woman who discovered that her husband was being unfaithful to her glued his penis to his leg with "superglue" while he was sleeping. He had to have an operation to get it unstuck. (1980)

Unconfirmed. This is a classic example of the "revenge" rumor, a theme shared by the stories of the stolen Mrs. Fields cookie recipe (page 122) and the fifty-dollar Porsche (page 197). Details of the wife's discovery of her husband's unfaithfulness are often added to the telling, and sometimes she seduces her husband and does the sticky deed while he has a full erection, greatly increasing his agony when the glue sets.

In all probability, the story is just a modern cautionary tale with no basis in fact. Jan Harold Brunvand discusses it as an urban legend in his book *The Choking Doberman*. We've found no news stories or medical reports of such marital sabotage, but superglue is powerful stuff, and the incident, or one similar, just might have really happened. When the glue first appeared on the market (superglue is a generic brand name for quick-bonding adhesives made with cyanoacrylate ester), many doctors became alarmed over the possibility that children could hurt themselves by misusing the glue. The November 1973 issue of *Consumer Reports* warned that "A handyman or child...who spilled a drop of this product on a finger and then touched an eyelid could end up with his finger stuck to his eyelid or with his eyelids cemented together." Consumer packages of superglue are printed with large-type warnings about the danger of bonding fingers or eyelids together. We haven't conducted any tests, but it would appear that an enraged wife could do some real damage to her husband with a few carefully placed drops of superglue.

A similar story, with the tables turned, has the wife as the unfaithful partner and the husband as the perpetrator of the vengeful deed. In this tale, the husband, a cement-truck operator, stops by his house during his usual working hours. He notices an unusual car in the driveway, a convertible, and peers through the bedroom window only to see his wife having sex with another man. Furious, he gets back in his truck, stews for a moment, then backs it into the driveway, lowers the chute, and fills the convertible with cement.

Again, it's an entertaining story, and it just might have happened somewhere, sometime. But we've never seen a news account, police report, or insurance claim to substantiate it, and we're pretty sure we never will.

ACKNOWLEDGMENTS

WE COULD NEVER HAVE WRITTEN this book without the contributions of many friends, rumormongers, and experts. Particular thanks are due to Richard Maurer, Ty Danco, Jeff Stone, Ellen Morgan, and Leon Rosenman for their elephant-like memories and their ears for good stories. Gerry Howard and Polly Cone gave enlightened editorial advice; and Terry White at NASA, Jan Harold Brunvand, and Jan Tucker were especially helpful in our search for the truth behind the stories. Thanks also to Paul Krassner, Sig Roos, Roger Manley, Tim Reach, David E. Pinto, Herbert A. Biern, Alphonzo Robon, John Wade, Judy Stratton, O. V. Barlow, Jeff Mariotte, Christopher C. Chalifoux, David Pitts, Michael G. Mears, Harvey Pulliam-Krager, Pete Kelly, Michael Norton, Pat Muller, Lee Ann Delaino, Dudley W. Sanders, Mark Szorady, Cassandra MacLean, Lisa Immel, Marc A. Catone, Terence Mahoney, Les Nirenberg, Louise Love, Terence Hines, Warren Marchioni, Tom Butler, Susan Wood, Peter DeWeese, Charlotte Ball, Bob Vagias, Lynde Kelley, Tracy Bruce, Paul Hanson, Rick Rader, Jonathon Bravard, Muffy Prenosil, Eli M. Rosenbaum, and George R. Lang, Jr.

INDEX

AC/DC, 10, 98–99

Addams, Jane, 101–3, 106

Alexian Brothers Hospital, 57–59

Anheuser-Busch, 133–34

Ark of the covenant, 54–56

Bacall, Lauren, 79–81

Barnett, Doris, 116–17

Beatles, 47, 84–85, 109–11

Belgian babies, hands cut off, 167–70

Bermuda Triangle, 35–39

Birthday song, 108

Blackout babies, 10, 113–15

Black socks, 89–90

Body in vat, 182–85

Break dancing, 82–84

Buffy, character on "Family Affair," 83

Butane lighters, 8, 187–90

Cabbage Patch Kid doll, 95

Calvi, Roberto, 61–62

Cat in bag, 119–21

Cement-truck driver's revenge, 200

Churchill, Winston, 151–54

Church's Fried Chicken, 137–39

Citizen Kane, 47–48

Clones, 14–16, 43–44

Coolidge, Calvin, 89–90

Coors, Adolph, Company, 133–34

Corpse in vat, 182–85

Crawford, Joan, 76–77

Cyclops, U.S.S., 36–37

Dammit doll, 94

Danger triangle, 179

Davis, Adelle, 67–68

Davis, Jefferson, 165–66

Death car, 198

Devil baby, 101–6

Doctorow, E. L., 128

Draft, Vietnam, 10–11, 140–41

DuBorg Hall, St. Louis University, 59

Duquesne Light Company, 191

Eastwood, Clint, 8, 77–78

Eggs, balanced at equinox, 116

Exorcism, 57–59

Exploding lighters, 187–90

FBI secret files, 142–45

FCC plan to ban religious broadcasting, 8, 53–54

Fields, Mrs., cookie recipe, 122–24
$50 Porsche, 197
Fixx, Jim, 69–70
Flight 19, 38–39
Ford Motor Company, 195–96
Fort Peck Dam, 112–13
Frehley, Ace, 96–97

Garbage strike, 118–19
Gibbons, Euell, 68–69
Guillotine, 29
Gun control, 133–34

Happy Birthday song, 108
Harvard Medical School, 9, 23–24
Hauptmann, Bruno Richard, 90–91
Heinz, H. J., Co., 25
Hoover, J. Edgar, 142–45
Hoover Dam, 112
Hubbard, L. Ron, 87–88
Hull House, 101–3, 106

Jackson, Jesse, 134–35
Jackson, Michael, 7–8, 82
Jersey Devil, 103–5
Jesus Christ, 48–52
Jockey shorts, 8–9, 177–78
John Paul I (pope), 59–62

Kennedy, John F., 136

Kidnapped child, 185–87
Kiss, 10, 96–97
Korvette, E. J., department store, 130
Kosher symbols, 131–32
Ku Klux Klan, 137

Lady slipper, 127
Lamborghini automobile company, 31–32
Laurel, Stan, 8, 77–78
Lee, Bruce, 65–67
Lincoln, Abraham, 47, 165–66
Lindbergh, Charles, 90–91
Lolo slaves, 174
Lost day, 8, 44–46
Lottery, California, 116–17
Lusitania, 151–54

Mammoth, 14–16
Mary Celeste, 36
Mathers, Gerry, 82
Mattel toy company, 175–76
McCartney, Paul, 84–85
Medina Air Force Base, 146
Michelob beer, 180
Mikey, of Life cereal commercials, 82
Miller, Glenn, 9, 85–87
Model kits, 33–34
Monroe, Marilyn, 9
Montreal Botanical Garden, 195
Morrison, Jim, 97

Mouse in soft drink, 181-82

"Mr. Ed" theme song, 10, 107

M16 rifle, 175–76

Mummies, Egyptian, 17–22

Mummy wheat, 13–14

Naked Came the Stranger, 128–29

NASA, discovery of lost day, 8, 44–46

Nautilus, U.S.S., 33–34

Nixon, Richard, 142–45, 150

Nuclear weapons, accidents involving, 146–49

Nursery rhymes, 92–93

Peace symbol, 99–101

Pearl Harbor, 155–61

Peggy Lawton Kitchens, 123

Philadelphia Experiment, 39–42

Pimples, danger of popping, 179

Praying mantis, 126–27

Presley, Elvis, 9

Procter & Gamble, 9–10, 106

Pryor, Richard, 189–90

Rand Corporation, 150

Red Cross, 171–72

Reeves, George, 8, 63–64

Remarque, Erich Maria, 129

Revell toy company, 33–34

Ribeiro, Alfonso, 82-84

Rickover, Hyman, 33–34

"Ring Around the Rosy," 92–93

Roosevelt, Franklin D., health of, 161–64; knowledge of attack on Pearl Harbor, 155–61

Rorvick, David, 43

St. Joseph's aspirin, 82–83

Satanism, 9–10, 96–107

Scientology, Church of, 87–88

Secret cities, 26–28

Secret Jewish tax, 131–32

Seeds, longevity of, 13–14

Sewers, flooding of, 10, 125

Shriver, Sargent, 136

Shroud dress, 192

Simmons, Gene, 96–97

Simmons, Richard, 81

Sinatra, Frank, 107

Sindona, Michele, 61–62

Skinner, B. F., 72–75

Snake in coat, 194–96

Soft contact lenses, 190–92

Sound recording, 47–48

Spider in dashboard, 195–96

Stealth fighter model, 34

Stroh Brewery Company, 134–35

Stuart, Charles Edward, 166–67

Super Bowl, 10, 125

Superglue, 9, 199-200
Superman, 8, 63–64

———————

Tanks, air-conditioned, 173
Tattoed draftee, 10–11, 140–41
Testor Corp., 34
Thumb in soup, 182
Thumb in tobacco, 180–82
"Tonight" show, 123–24
Troll doll, 94

———————

Union Pacific Railroad, 187–90
United Parcel Service, 191–92
United States government and agencies, rumors about, 8, 39–42, 44–46, 53–54, 126, 142–45

Vatican, 48–50, 59–62
Victoria (queen of England), 71–72
Von Bülow, Claus, 70
Von Bülow, Hans, 48

———————

Wartime rumors, World War I, 151–54, 167–72; World War II, 155–61, 171–74; Vietnam, 10–11, 140–41, 175–76
Welders, accidents involving, 187–92
Williams, Andy, 79–81

———————

Yesterday and Today album, 109–11

Request for Rumors

WE ARE CONTINUING our rumor research, and would appreciate any help that you can give us. If you hear or remember any interesting rumors that we haven't discussed, please send us a note. It would be helpful if you let us know the year in which you first heard each rumor—as closely as you can remember.

We will share your letters with other rumor and folklore researchers, and we'll draw on them if we do a sequel to this book.

Please address your correspondence to us at:

Steam Press
15 Warwick Road
Watertown, MA 02172